LIVING IN THE
70s

WHAT ABOUT ME?

G. S. WILLMOTT

CONTENTS

1970	3
1971	9
1972	23
1973	54
1974	74
1975	93
1976	110
1977	132
1978	154
1979	181

*Why is the 1970s referred to as the **Me Decade**?*
During the 1970s as things began to wind down and feel more peaceful after a turbulent decade, people became more interested in bettering themselves. Individualism got more important as people became dissatisfied with wars and politics. ... Since the 1970s were all about expressing oneself, they were dubbed the "Me Decade".

1970

CHAPTER 1

Best Picture 1970

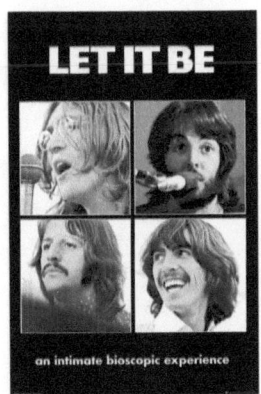

No 1 Record 1970

January 1

Me 1970

I turned eighteen, I was the first baby boy born in Victoria in 1952. The other significant event was that I started university studying Business Studies. Why? Not because I had the ambition to become another Warren Buffet or Maynard Keynes. Business Studies required only sixteen hours of lectures a week, giving me more time for activities such as surfing and other leisure activities that are best not mentioned.

My much-loved Kombi Van

Other significant events in 1970

The Cambodian Incursion AKA Invasion

This was a series of military operations in Cambodia by South Vietnamese and United States forces. The motivation was to defeat the approximately 40,000 North Vietnamese troops including the Viet Cong who were stationed in Cambodia. They established several bases, enabling them to conduct military operations into South Vietnam.

The USA was heading towards withdrawing from the war and enabling the South Vietnamese army to manage the war effort in their own right. The invasion was designed to eliminate the cross-border threat.

Prince Sihanouk Cambodia's Head of State was deposed in March 1970 and was replaced by Lon Noi, a Cambodian general.

Prince Sihanouk

The South Vietnamese along with Cambodian troops captured several towns, but the North Vietnamese were able to escape the cordon. The US and South Vietnamese offensive was partly successful, but the majority of the North Vietnamese escaped.

Richard Nixon was looking for a win; he was under enormous pressure from not only the Democrats but also his own party, the Republicans.

In 1970, 6,173 American soldiers died in Vietnam. There were protests taking place all over America and indeed the world.

With the invasion of Cambodia, he thought could win the approval of the American people.

USA Bombing Cambodia

Richard Nixon on national television justifying his decision

Protest in Washington 1970

Protest in Melbourne Australia - Can you see me? I was there.

1971

CHAPTER 2

Best Picture 1971

Number 1 Record 1971

1971 was my second year at university. Significant events in my life included purchasing a new surfboard and a pair of Ugg Boots. I was the first person to wear these fashion icons on campus.

I spent Easter with the surfing crew at Wilson's Promontory.

Wilson's Promontory

Glamping at The Prom
I'm the one lying down.

Other significant events in 1971

Uganda

The 1971 Uganda coup was a military coup d'état executed by the Ugandan military, led by General Idi Amin, against the government of President Milton Obote on January 25, 1971. The seizure of power took place while Obote was abroad attending the Commonwealth Heads of Government Meeting in Singapore.

General Idi Amin

Initially Amin was pro-western, enjoying support from Britain and other western countries, including Israel.

His allegiances soon changed, and he became a strong ally of Colonel Gaddafi, President of Libya, and of the Soviet Union, particularly East Germany.

Ironically Uganda became a member of the United Nations Commission on Human Rights.

The United Kingdom broke off diplomatic relations in 1977.

Amin declared to the world that he had defeated Britain and added CBE to his many titles, all self-appointed.

CBE stood for "Conqueror of the British Empire".

As the 70s progressed there was increased western unrest against his persecution of some ethnic groups and political dissidents.

His reputation was not enhanced when he supported terrorists who had hijacked a commercial flight and subsequently gave the hijackers safe passage.

His next illegal action was attempting to annex Tanzania's Kagera Region in 1978.

Amin had bitten off more than he could chew and the Tanzanian President, Julius Nyerere, invaded Uganda, capturing the capital, Kampala and ousting Amin from power. Amin went into exile first to Libya, then

Iraq. He finally settled in Saudi Arabia where the royal family protected him. He died in 2003.

Idi Amin was a despot responsible for massive human rights abuses.

It is estimated he was responsible for the deaths of 500,000 of his own people.

Amin gave himself several titles throughout his reign, including His Excellency President for Life, Field Marshal Al Hadji, Doctor Idi Amin, VC, DSO, MC, Lord of All the Beasts of the Earth and Fishes of the Sea, and Conqueror of the British Empire in Africa in General and Uganda in Particular.

The Idi Amin quotes listed below were taken from books, newspapers, and magazines reporting on his speeches, interviews, and telegrams to other state officials.

"I am not a politician but a professional soldier. I am, therefore, a man of few words and I have been brief through my professional career."

  Idi Amin, President of Uganda, from his first speech to the Ugandan nation in January 1971.

"Germany is the place where when Hitler was the prime minister and supreme commander, he burned over six million Jews. This is because Hitler and all German people knew that Israelis are not people who are working in the interest of the world and that is why they burned the Israelis alive with gas in the soil of Germany."

  Idi Amin, President of Uganda, part of a telegram sent to Kurt Waldheim, UN Secretary-General, and Golda Meir, Israeli premier, on 12 Sept 1972.

"I am the hero of Africa."

  Idi Amin, President of Uganda, as quoted in *Newsweek* 12 March 1973.

"While wishing you a speedy recovery from the Watergate affair, may I, Excellency, assure you of my highest respect and regard."

President Idi Amin of Uganda, message to U.S. President Richard M. Nixon, on July 4, 1973, as reported in The New York Times, 6 July 1973.

"Sometimes people mistake the way I talk for what I am thinking. I never had any formal education—not even a nursery school certificate. But, sometimes I know more than PhDs because as a military man I know how to act, I am a man of action."
Idi Amin as quoted in Thomas and Margaret Melady's *Idi Amin Dada: Hitler in Africa*, Kansas City, 1977.

"I do not want to be controlled by any superpower. I myself consider myself the most powerful figure in the world, and that is why I do not let any superpower control me."
Idi Amin, President of Uganda, as quoted in Thomas and Margaret Melady's *Idi Amin Dada: Hitler in Africa*, Kansas City, 1977.

"Like the Prophet Mohammed, who sacrificed his life and his property for the good of Islam, I am ready to die for my country."
From Radio Uganda and attributed to Idi Amin in 1979, as reported in "Amin, Living by the Gun, Under the Gun, " *The New York Times*, 25 March 1979.

February 1971

Tricky Dicky

A sound-activated tape-recording system was installed in the Oval Office. The tapes were open reel, designed to capture audio transmitted by telephone taps and concealed microphones. Nixon was so pleased he ordered the expansion into other rooms in the White House and Camp David.
This would eventually lead to his downfall.

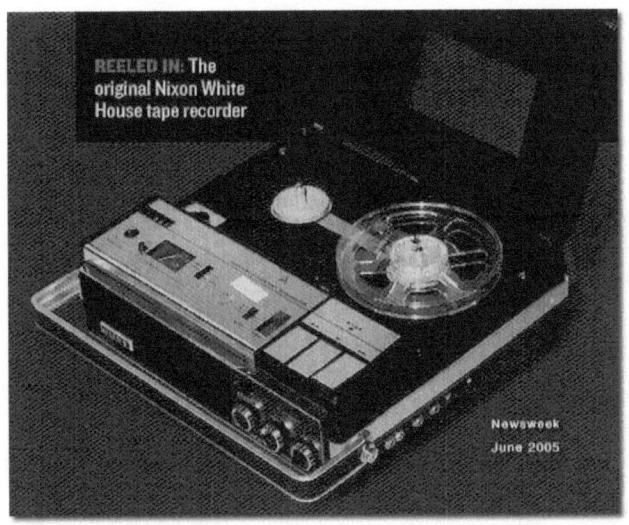

REELED IN: The original Nixon White House tape recorder

Newsweek
June 2005

The White House tapes were recordings of conversations between Richard Nixon and members of his administration. He also recorded his own family members.

March 1971

The Bangladesh Liberation War

India was partitioned in 1947. Britain reluctantly let the "Jewel in the Crown" go.

Pakistan was created as a separate country for Muslims. India was predominantly Hindu, and this separation of the Bengali society based on religion created enormous tensions between the two countries.

East Pakistan was physically separated from West Pakistan by 1000 miles.

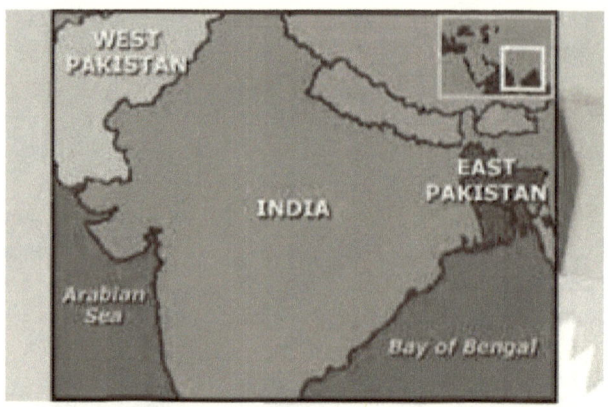

Religion, decided the borders. It was the catalyst for a terrible disaster.

From the beginning, the Pakistani ruling elite, who were controlled by the military, dominated every aspect of West Pakistan, including politically, culturally and economically. Disillusionment became endemic. The West Pakistanis wanted control over their region.

In the first-ever national Parliamentary elections, the Bengali nationalist forces led by Bangabandhu Sheikh Mujibur Rahman won a landslide victory. Consequently his party, the Awami League, became the majority party in the whole of Pakistan. However, in an attempt to crush this nationalistic movement, the Pakistani Military Junta unleashed a systematic genocide against the Bengali people on the fateful night of March 25, 1971. The Junta received support only from a handful of religion-based local parties and religious fundamentalists. The Pakistani rampage in the nine months of 1971 resulted in the worst genocide since the Second World War, and an estimated 3 million people were killed, some 278,000 women were raped and 10 million had to take refuge in neighbouring India. A government in exile was quickly formed and the resistance started becoming more and more coordinated. Young people from the villages and students took military training and the Mukti Bahini (freedom fighters) backed the occupation forces under 11 Sectors, adopted guerrilla tactics and kept the Pakistani army in a harassed and indefensible state. By September these half-trained young men had infiltrated deep inside Bangladesh and a large part of the country was virtually self-ruled.

On December 3, after Pakistan attacked and bombed airfields in the western part of India, the Allied Command of the Indian Army and the Muktibahini (Bangladesh Freedom Fighters) was formed. They started the formal armed assault. On December 16, 1971, the Pakistani Armed Forces ignominiously surrendered to this Allied Command and independent Bangladesh was born as a democratic and secular state.

To put it into perspective a total of 1,353,000 people died during the Vietnam War over nine years.

In nine months over three million Bangladeshi citizens were killed.

Concert for Bangladesh

Ravi Shankar, revered sitar musician and friend of the Beatles, was a native of Bangladesh. He was devastated by the carnage and the resulting famine in his homeland. He called his good friend George Harrison with a plea for help.

George was very sympathetic to the cause. He invited Ravi to his home, *Friar Park*, at Henley on Thames for dinner with the purpose of discussing what George could do to help.

Friar Park

Sitting at the dining table was George, his wife Patti, Ravi and Klaus Voormann the record producer. The meal consisted of minestrone soup, lasagne and ice cream.

'George, I am very sad about what is happening in my country. I know it doesn't really concern you in England but I know you are a true humanitarian. You are probably not aware that 3 million people have been killed, some 278,000 women have been raped and over 10 million of my people have had to take refuge in India. All this in nine months.'

George, his wife and his guest Klaus were all moved by Ravi's description of Bangladesh's plight.

'Ravi I'm going to try and help you. Leave it with me.'

George manned the phone and over three months arranged for some of his good friends to take part in two concerts on the same day at Madison Square Gardens.

Some, such as John Lennon, had previous commitments that could not be broken.

George put together a supergroup of artists including Ringo Starr, Bob Dylan, Eric Clapton, Billy Preston, Leon Russel and Bad Finger. Ravi Shankar and Ali Akbar Khan performed the opening set. Both were Bangladeshi.

The two concerts attracted 40,000 people, generating $250,000 in receipts, which went to the Bangladesh Relief Fund administered by UNICEF.

The album and film generated a further $12,000,000.

The world had discovered Bangladesh.

July 9
Kissinger's Secret Trip

Henry Kissinger quietly boarded a Boeing 707 at an airbase in Pakistan.

He was to become the first US official to visit the People's Republic of China since its founding in 1949.

The mission was codenamed 'Operation Marco Polo' after the 13th-century Venetian explorer who spent 17 years in China.

The atmosphere was tense, but when Kissinger met with Chinese Premier Zhou Enlai that afternoon Kissinger's trepidation abated. Unbeknownst to Kissinger, then-President Richard Nixon had just made the "Five-Power World" speech in which he asserted that China would become a superpower.

Zhou provided Kissinger and his team with printouts of Nixon's speech so that they could get up to speed and declared that China did not have ambitions to rival America on the global stage.

The meeting lasted from 4pm until nearly midnight, then the following day Kissinger toured the Palace Museum. A date was set for Nixon to visit China and Kissinger departed Beijing on July 11.

Kissinger meets Mao

Kissinger given chopsticks lessons

Welcome China goodbye Taiwan

On Oct. 25, 1971, the United Nations General Assembly voted to admit the People's Republic of China (mainland China) and to expel the Republic of China (Taiwan). The Communist P.R.C. therefore assumed the R.O.C.'s place in the General Assembly as well as its place as one of the five permanent members of the U.N. Security Council.

Chinese Delegation Celebrating UN Membership

1972

CHAPTER 3

Best Picture 1972

No 1 Record 1972

This was a significant year for me. My parents moved from Melbourne to the Gold Coast in Queensland. They had established a very successful business and were considered wealthy. Unfortunately, wealth doesn't buy you health. The medical advice was for Sam, my father, to move to a warmer climate or he would die prematurely. At the ages of 52 and 50, they handed the business over to my brother John who was six years my senior and moved to a place with a strange name; Nobby's Beach.

My parents purchased an investment house in Bentleigh in the same street I was brought up in and that's where I lived. I paid them rent which was partly covered by my housemates who came and went. There were periods when I was the only tenant and covering the rent was difficult.

This brought on my first episode of depression.

My mother flew down and advised me to stop taking the pills that were prescribed. She said she would rent the house out and she slipped me a significant amount of cash and told me to take off in my Kombi and surf until I felt better.

I, with two surfing mates, did just that.

We drove to Queensland, surfing up the New South Wales coast. We stayed on the Gold Coast for a while then went up to Noosa Heads where we lived for three months. We then travelled up to Cairns then back to Noosa for another month. We drove back to Melbourne and then I made my way to South Australia where I worked on a farm on the York Peninsula.

By this time I felt good. I drove back to Melbourne, had a haircut, and got a job as an accountant starting in January 1973.

Other significant events in 1972

Pierre Hotel Robbery

The most successful hotel robbery in history was the Pierre Hotel. Six men dressed in tuxedos robbed the safe-deposit boxes of the luxury hotel in New York, taking over an estimated $30 million in cash and jewellery. Only two of the robbers were caught and jailed.

The two men were enjoying a whisky at the King Cole Bar located at 2 East 55th Street. Sam Nalo and Robert Comfort were friends and business colleagues. Their business was burglary and armed robbery. Christie "the tic" Furnari joined them at the far end of the bar. Anyone who knew them kept their distance. Sam and Rob were members of the Rochester

Crime Family while Christie was associated with the Lucchese Crime Family. The purpose of the get-together was to finalise the plan for the Pierre Hotel heist prior to letting the rest of the gang in on the plan.

Pierre Hotel New York

'Well boys, we know we can get away with it. We proved that when we robbed that Italian dame with the big tits,' said Rob.

'That's true, Sam. We pocketed over a million in jewellery. By the way her name was Sophia Loren.'

'Let's not get carried away boys— we broke into her apartment. The jewels weren't in a safety deposit box,' said Sam.

Nalo and Comfort were the planners of the robbery. The other members were aware there was a job to be done but had no idea what it was. They were all due to meet at Nalo's nightclub, the *Port Said*, on December 30th. All would be revealed.

The *Port Said*, located at 257 West 29th Street, was in the heart of the original belly dance belt. The *Port Said* is essentially Greek, but you can find other Mediterraneans such as Italians frequenting this popular spot. Nalo gathered the gang together and announced the intended target.

The gang consisted of:

Robert "Bobby" Germaine; a member of the Lucchese crime family. He was an expert safebreaker. His job was to break open the safety deposit boxes. He didn't need to crack the hotel's safe, as the boxes were stored in an open vault.

Ali-Ben, a hit man, was on the team but they hoped he wouldn't be needed. He was a member of the Albanian Mafia.

Finally, Al Green, Ali Ben's brother-in-law, made up the numbers.

The gang arrived at *The Pierre* at 3:50 a.m. on January 2, 1972. Ten minutes later Green, dressed in a chauffeur's uniform, drove a black Cadillac limousine up to the hotel's entrance. Green got out and informed the security guard that he was there to pick up Dr Foster's party. The security guard called the front desk to confirm Dr Foster was a hotel guest.

Comfort had booked and paid for a room using Dr Foster as an alias.

The guard unlocked the door. Once Green had access he pulled a magnum out from his coat and held the guard at gunpoint while the other gang members entered the luxury hotel. Green stayed outside with the guard and kept a lookout.

The gang members quickly rounded up the hotel staff and instructed them to lie face-down on the floor where all were handcuffed. They had nineteen hostages.

To ensure they weren't recognised, all the gang members wore disguises; none more ludicrous than Nalo who wore a huge wig, fake nose and glasses.

Nalo persuaded the hotel auditor to provide the index cards so that the boxes could be matched to the depositors. They only broke into the boxes of guests they recognised.

The burglars were polite at all times and addressed the hostages as sir or miss.

The scene of the robbery

The robbery took two and a half hours. That is how long Bobby G and Comfort took to break into a quarter of the 208 locked boxes in the vault.

Before they left the hotel, Comfort warned the hostages that if they recognised any of the gang and informed the police they would be shot and killed.

Having said that, he gave each staff member a twenty-dollar bill. He did exclude the security guards on principle.

Ultimately, Comfort and Nalo were arrested after the $750,000 Harry Winston necklace was found in the possession of a Detroit mobster who also happened to be an FBI informant. They were the only two members of the crew who were ever charged with The Pierre Hotel robbery and they took a plea deal—which, according to the team's only surviving member, was arranged via a bribe of $500,000 from the Lucchese crime family to a Manhattan Supreme Court Justice. They each served 19 months in prison for the robbery.

Hewlett Packard

The first scientific hand-held calculator is released to the market at a price of $395.

It would be U.S.$2,663 in today's dollars

January 6

U.S. President Richard Nixon ordered the development of the Space Shuttle Program.

Queen Margrethe II of Denmark succeeded her father King Frederick IX on the throne of Denmark, the first Queen of Denmark since 1412 and the first Danish monarch not named Frederick since 1513.
I think it was wise not to name her Queen Frederick.

January

Shoichi Yokoi, a sergeant in the Imperial Japanese Army during the Second World War, was discovered in his hideout in January 1972. He was unaware that the war had ended, and Japan had been defeated.

January 26

The Aboriginal Tent Embassy was established on the lawn of Parliament House in Canberra.

Pakistan withdraws from the Commonwealth

Mariner 9 sends back pictures of Mars

Sunday Bloody Sunday

In January 1972 the Prime Minister of Northern Ireland, Brian Falkner, banned marches in Northern Ireland until December that year.

Not to be denied, the Northern Ireland Civil Rights Association (NICRA) organised a march protesting against internment without trial. The march was organised to take place on January 22

The protesters marched on an internment camp at Magilligan Beach near Derry.

The infamous Parachute Regiment was there to greet them. The PR had a reputation for brutality.

The use of rubber bullets and batons was criticised by police and regular army officers in attendance.

Television and newspaper reports were very critical of the PR's behaviour.

Despite the ban, another march was organised the following Sunday in Derry: a day that would go down in history.

Saturday 29 January

32 Anne Street, Brandywell, Londonderry

'Hey Dad, are you still intending to go on the march tomorrow?' asked Charlie.

'Why wouldn't I? It's something I believe in. You shouldn't be able to lock up someone without a trial. I'd march every bloody Sunday if I had to.'

'I've been giving it some thought and even though I'm a bit worried after what happened at the beach last weekend, I've decided to join you.'

'Good lad, I'm proud of you, son. Don't worry about the cops and the army; they will have learned their lesson.'

The 1st Battalion, Parachute Regiment were ordered to travel to Derry with orders to arrest possible rioters.

The protesters planned to march into the city centre where they would hold a rally. Approximately 15,000 people set off at 2.45 p.m.

As the march neared the city centre, police barriers halted them. The organisers changed their plans and headed for Free Derry Corner where they now would hold the rally.

Some militant protesters broke away and began throwing rocks at the soldiers manning the barriers. The soldiers reacted with rubber bullets, tear gas and water cannons. Such actions were quite common in Northern Ireland but things escalated when soldiers shot Damian Donaghy and John Johnston, both unarmed civilians.

At 4.07 p.m. the paratroopers were ordered to scale the barriers and arrest the rioters. While some troops were in armoured vehicles, most were on foot. The paratroopers chased people down Rossville Street against the orders of Brigadier MacLellan. The result was that rioters and peaceful marchers merged.

Young William Nash was just standing beside a three-storey building. He was holding a fold up umbrella as rain was forecast. His dad had suggested they both should bring an umbrella. William didn't hear the shot. He just dropped to the footpath, dead before he hit the cement.

His father Alexander saw what happened and ran to his son's aid. He too was shot dead.

William and his father had worked together on the docks and now they died together. The family was now eleven.

The paratrooper who shot them thought the umbrellas were some type of weapon.

Fourteen innocent victims died that Sunday. No one was held responsible, despite a number of judicial inquiries.

February 21 -28

U.S. President Richard Nixon makes an eight-day visit to the People's Republic of China and meets Mao Zedong.
Why?
The U. S. ambassador explains the motivation for the visit.

'The reason for opening up China was for the U.S. to gain more leverage over relations with the Soviet Union. Resolving the Vietnam War was a particularly important factor. National Security Council staffer (and later U.S. Ambassador to China) Winston Lord noted:
First, an opening to China would give us more flexibility on the world scene generally. We wouldn't just be dealing with Moscow. We could deal with Eastern Europe, of course, and we could deal with China because the former Communist Bloc was no longer a bloc. Kissinger wanted more flexibility, generally. Secondly, by opening relations with China we would catch Russia's attention and get more leverage on them through playing this obvious China card. The idea would be to improve relations with Moscow, hoping to stir a little bit of its paranoia by dealing with China, never getting so engaged with China that we would turn Russia into a hostile enemy but enough to get the attention of the Russians. This effort worked dramatically after Kissinger's secret trip to China. Thirdly, Kissinger and Nixon wanted to get help in resolving the Vietnam War. By dealing with Russia and with China we hoped to put pressure on Hanoi to negotiate seriously. At a maximum, we tried to get Russia and China to slow down the provision of aid to North Vietnam somewhat. More realistically and at a minimum, we sought to persuade Russia and China to encourage Hanoi to make a deal with the United States and give Hanoi a sense of isolation because their two big patrons were dealing with us. Indeed, by their willingness to engage in summit meetings with us, with Nixon going to China in February 1972, and to Moscow in May

1972, the Russians and Chinese were beginning to place a higher priority on their bilateral relations with us than on their dealings with their friends in Hanoi.'

Nixon meets Mao

March 2

Pioneer 10

The Pioneer 10 spacecraft was launched by NASA at Cape Kennedy. Pioneer 10 was the first spacecraft to leave our solar system.

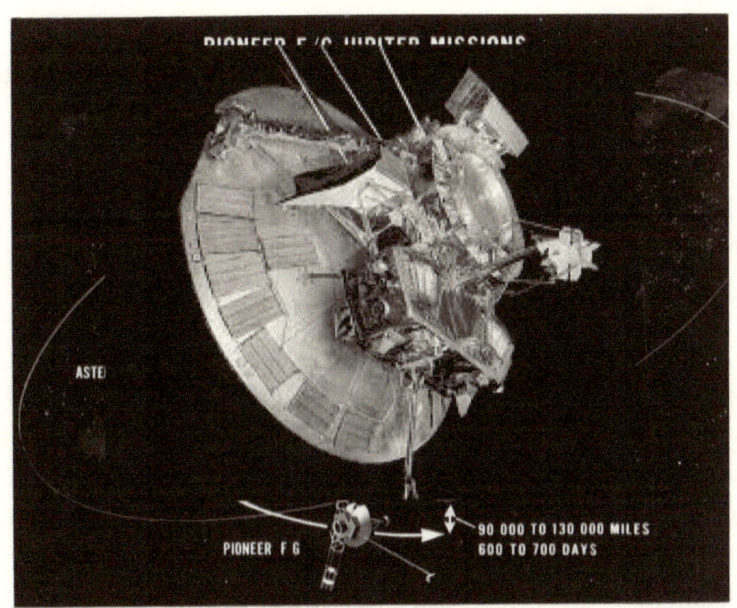

Pioneer 10 AKA F

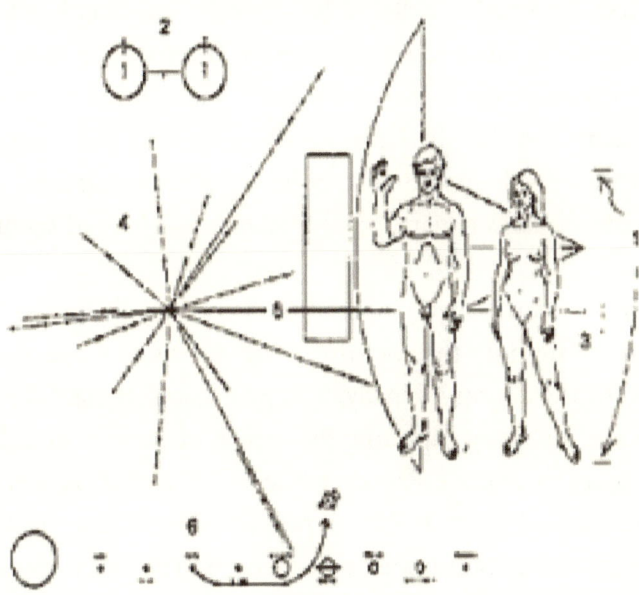

This plaque was attached to the spacecraft to introduce ourselves to extraterrestrials

March 13

Following the United States' lead, the United Kingdom and The People's Republic of China exchanged ambassadors after 22 years.

March 30

The Easter Offensive Vietnam

At the beginning of 1972, North Vietnam prepared for a major invasion of South Vietnam known as the Easter Offensive. North Vietnam contended that the offensive would prove to be the downfall of South Vietnam. However, it severely underestimated the resolve of both South Vietnam and the United States to prevent a communist takeover.

North Vietnam planned the Easter Offensive with a number of factors in mind. First, North Vietnam believed that the South Vietnamese forces, known as the Army of the Republic of Vietnam (South Vietnamese), were not capable of defending the nation. This theory was developed following the catastrophic loss the South Vietnamese suffered during Operation Lam Son 719 in Laos in 1971. It was also backed by the observation that the United States' policy of Vietnamization, or turning the war over to South Vietnam, would fail due to a lack of training by the USA.

Also, North Vietnam believed that the Vietnamese living within South Vietnam would support the overthrow of the nation and the national reunification of the country. Finally, it hoped that a successful invasion of South Vietnam, including capturing the capital of Saigon, would convince American voters to remove President Richard Nixon from office during the 1972 presidential election. Nixon proved to be a thorn in the side of North Vietnam; the nation hoped that George McGovern would win the election and would then remove all American troops from Vietnam. The North Vietnamese reasoning was wrong.

North Vietnam launched its invasion on March 30, 1972. Roughly 120,000 North Vietnamese troops, a mixture of the People's Army of

Vietnam, North Vietnamese and remaining elements of the National Liberation Front (NLF), moved into South Vietnam.

North Vietnamese Tanks Invading the South

The North Vietnamese strategy was a three-pronged approach: a direct attack across the Demilitarized Zone, an invasion into the Central Highlands and the capturing of the city of An Loc.

The first wave of the North Vietnamese (People's Army of Vietnam) troops reached the province of Quang Tri, just across the Demilitarized Zone, on March 31. Within a day, the North Vietnamese had administered a devastating defeat to the South Vietnamese division stationed in the area. By the end of April, Quang Tri City had been captured by North Vietnamese

The North Vietnamese then moved toward the city of Hue.

Quang Tri City

Sensing an imminent defeat, the President of South Vietnam, Nguyen Van Thieu, quickly replaced the South Vietnamese commanders within the region. The gamble worked as the South's forces regrouped and mounted a counteroffensive beginning in May. With assistance from American air and sea firepower, the South Vietnamese halted the North Vietnamese movement toward Hue and recaptured Quang Tri in September.

North Vietnam's second wave of the offensive was eerily similar to that of the first. The North invaded the Central Highlands region on April 12. The goal was to capture the provinces of Kontum and Pleiku, as well as divide South Vietnam in half at Route 19. At the onset of the engagement, the South Vietnamese took significant losses, and vital cities such as Dak To quickly fell to the North Vietnamese forces.

The third and final prong of the offensive focused on the North Vietnamese capturing An Loc.

The Viet Cong and North Vietnamese bombarded An Loc with everything that it had, but the besieged South Vietnamese forces, with the help of precise American artillery, fought valiantly. After over 90 days of combating the enemy, reinforcements arrived. The South launched a counter offensive and swiftly defeated the Viet Cong and North Vietnamese forces.

Battle of An Loc

December 1972

Washington DC

Richard Nixon was sitting at the famous Resolute Desk. Many presidents before him and after him sat at the same desk with pride.

Nixon had hoped to end the Vietnam War, but things were not going America's way.

His foray into Laos the previous year endeavouring to destroy the Ho Chi Minh trail had failed miserably.

His Secretary of State, William Rogers, was advising him.

John Ehrlichman and his Defence Minister Melvin Laird advised that the only way to beat the communists was to bomb the living daylights out of them.

Operation Linebacker was devised to drop over 20,000 tons of high explosive over Hanoi predominantly to break the enemy's spirit.

Café Pho Co

Hang Buom and his wife Ha ran a café, *Café Pho Co*, in the centre of Hanoi. Their two children, Chi, a twelve-year-old girl, and An, a fourteen-year-old boy, helped their parents when they were not attending school.

'I'm hopeful this wretched war will be over soon. The Paris peace talks have been going for some time now,' said Hang Buom.

'I hope you are right, my husband. Who can forget the bombing of 1966? I was sure we would all die.'

'It looks like a good crowd today. Maybe the Christians are out celebrating Christmas.'

'True. Do you know how many Christians there are in Vietnam?'

'About seven million, apparently.'

'Chi asked me if she will receive a present for Christmas this year.'

'What did you tell her?'

'I explained we are communists and don't believe in Jesus.'

'How did she take it?'

'Pretty well. She just wanted a new dress. She didn't care about Christmas or Jesus.'

'When they both get home from school we'll treat them to a special cake.'

December 18
Guam Pacific

Captain Gary Woods briefed his five-man crew before take-off.

'Okay, boys, we are next to take off. We and the 86 other bombers are heading for Hanoi. We intend to blow the living daylights out of the Commies. If that doesn't make them surrender nothing will.'

The bomber force took six hours and fourteen minutes to reach Hanoi and began dropping over 20,000 tons of bombs.

Bombs Hits Hanoi

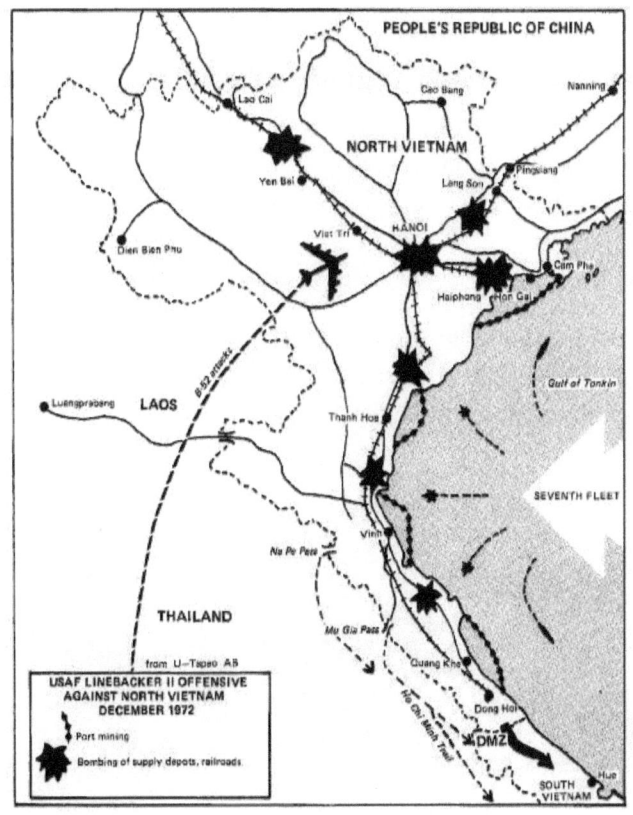

An and Chi were walking home from school when An stopped in his tracks.

'What's wrong, An?'

'Look up. What do you see?'

'Oh no.'

The two children saw American bombers blotting out the sky. Bombs began to fall on their beloved city. They ran to a Catholic church, hoping they would be safe.

The bombing lasted well over an hour and when the bombardment finished, An and Chi returned to their parents' café and home. As they approached their neighbourhood they realised it had been largely destroyed. They turned the corner and stared at the devastation they couldn't recognise as the café. They scrambled as fast as they could over the bombed-out buildings until they reached what they believed was their home. Their mother and father lay among the rubble. Both were dead.

A soldier approached the siblings and asked if they had a family. They informed him both their parents had been killed in the bombing.

'Do you have any living relatives?'

'We have an uncle who lives on a farm on the outskirts of Hanoi,' answered An.

'Come and show me where.'

An and Chi and the soldier made their way to the children's uncle's farm. Both children sobbed most of the way.

Total Destruction

They walked five miles, reaching Uncle Huynh's house at dusk.

Huynh was regarded as a wealthy farmer in the region, as his farm covered over 100 acres whereas most farms in the area were 10 acres or less.

'You two stay here while I talk to your uncle,' said Duc, the soldier.

'Hello, is there anybody home?'

There was no answer. Duc yelled louder. Finally, a distinctive looking man appeared.

'Who are you? I don't recall inviting anybody here tonight.'

'Excuse me, sir, but I have a most important subject to discuss with you.'

Duc explained what had happened to the children's parents and how he, their uncle, was their only living relative.

'I had two sons. Both were killed in the war. I don't believe I could take care of the children. I suggest you find them a suitable orphanage in Hanoi.'

'Your niece and nephew will be mortified. They have not only lost their parents, but they are now being rejected by their only living kin.'

'I have my reasons.'

Duc explained to the children that their uncle did not have room for them.

'Come, we will find an orphanage where you will be able to stay. They will look after you both.'

The only orphanage Duc knew was the Hanoi Orphanage. He led the children to the building that housed the institution. Duc was relieved to discover the building was undamaged.

He needed to return to barracks as he had already been away too long.

'I'm leaving you here. Just knock on the front door and explain your situation. Good luck.'

The children did as Duc instructed, and an older lady opened the door and ushered them in. After hearing their story, she accepted them both as orphans.

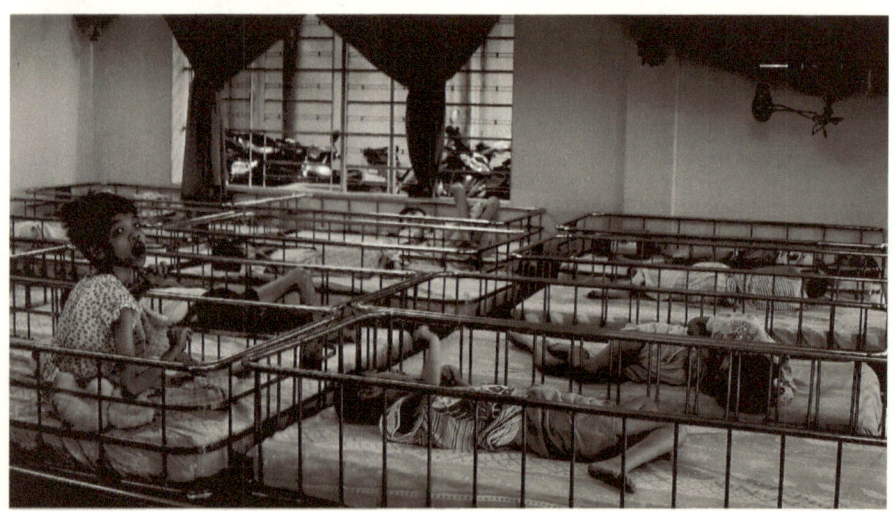

Dormitory

Luna Rover

July 31

Moon

Astronauts

John Young

Ken Mattingly

Charlie Duke

The rover was first used on 31 July 1971, during the Apollo 15 mission. This greatly expanded the range of the lunar explorers. Previous teams of astronauts were restricted to short walking distances around the landing site due to the bulky space suit equipment required to sustain life in the lunar environment.

Watergate Scandal

Watergate has become synonymous with any scandal around the globe. The "gate" suffix has been used to refer to local scandals in countries such as Argentina, Germany, South Korea, Hungary, Greece, Great Britain, Australia, and the former Yugoslavia.

The initial Watergate Scandal emanated in America when Richard Nixon was vying to become a second term President. Its genesis was June 1972 and it ended in controversy in 1974 when Richard Nixon resigned.

June 17, 1972

Frank Wills worked the midnight to 7 a.m. shift as a security guard at the Watergate Office Building in Washington, DC. Shortly after signing in on June 17, 1972, the 24-year-old Wills noticed something amiss. His entries into the Watergate's security log reveal that he found doors on levels B2 and B3 stuffed with paper. At 12:30 a.m., Wills "cut all lights out in hall" and began to investigate. When he found a door taped open, he called the DC police. It was just before 2 a.m.

So began the biggest scandal in U.S. presidential history.

Five burglars were arrested during the initial interrogation. A large sum of money was discovered on their persons. It was traced to the Nixon re-election campaign.

The Watergate scandal had been uncovered. It was linked to the break-in of the Democratic National Committee headquarters at the Watergate office building in Washington.

Watergate Complex

During the trials of the five burglars, further revelations were uncovered. As a result the House of Representatives approved the Judiciary Committee wide ranging authority to probe deeper into the matter. The U.S. Senate also created a Special Investigative Committee to investigate a possible cover-up by Richard Nixon. The Senate permitted live television coverage of the proceedings. This captured the interest of the American people.

Several witnesses testified that Nixon had approved plans to cover up his administration's involvement in the break-in.

It was also revealed that Nixon had approved a voice-activated taping system in the Oval Office.

Throughout the investigation the Nixon administration resisted the evidence.

As a result the House commenced the impeachment process against the President.

The U.S. Supreme Court ordered Nixon to release the Oval Office tapes to the investigation.

The tapes revealed that Nixon had conspired to cover up activities that occurred after the break-in and later tried to use federal officials to deflect the investigation.

The House Judiciary Committee approved three articles of impeachment against Nixon for obstruction of justice, abuse of power and contempt of Congress.

Nixon had no other choice; he resigned from office on August 9, 1974.

He was the only President in U.S. history to resign.

His successor Gerald Ford pardoned him.

Goodbye everyone

September 5

The Munich Massacre

The Essence of Terror

Summer Olympics 1972

West Germany was hoping 1972 games would eradicate the memory of Hitler's 1936 games.

However they would be remembered as the games where the terrorists demonstrated to the world their true colours. Members of the Israeli Olympic team were taken hostage, and some were murdered by Black September. BS was a terrorist group with ties to Yasser Arafat's Farah organisation.

By the end of the ordeal the terrorists had killed eleven Israeli athletes and coaches. One German police officer was killed.

Berlin played host to two Olympic games in the 20th century. Both will be remembered for the wrong reasons.

1973

CHAPTER 4

Best Picture

Number 1 Record

This was a year of insignificance for me. I was working as an Assistant
Accountant for a book distribution company. The only redeeming thing

about the job was that I could browse the bookshelves at lunchtime. Any book that took my fancy could be purchased with a 50% staff discount.

The other redeeming event was discovering trail bikes. A couple of old school friends had purchased trail bikes and invited me to have a go. I was hooked. I went out and bought one. We rode the tracks through the Black Spur Range in Victoria and practised Motocross on suburban tracks.

I had moved back into 2 McKittrick Road but this time I enjoyed the experience.

2 McKittrick Road

Me on the Trail

February 12

POWs Go Home

The year began well as the U.S. Government and her allies signed a Peace Accord with the North Vietnamese Government.

Henry Kissinger, acting as the Assistant for National Security to President Nixon, was the chief negotiator.

The accord required the U.S.A. to withdraw all troops from Vietnam. The agreement also specified for six hundred POWs to be released within sixty days of the American withdrawal.

This agreement would become known as Operation Homecoming.

The former prisoners were flown to Clark Air Base in the Philippines where they were processed, debriefed and physically examined.

POWs Flying Home

Two well-known POWs were John McCain and John Borling.
The doctors and psychologists were amazed at the resiliency of the majority of the men who had been released.

John Borling

John McCain

Borling and McCain decided to further their careers in the U.S. Air Force.

February 27

Bury My Heart at Wounded Knee
The Occupation

The second Wounded Knee began in February when approximately 22 Oglala Lakota (Sioux) Indians and their supporters seized and occupied the town of Wounded Knee in South Dakota. The town is located within the Pine Ridge Indian Reservation.

The protest resulted from the failure of the Oglala Sioux Civil Rights Organisation (OSCRO) to impeach the tribal chief Richard Wilson, who they accused of corruption and abuse of any opposition to his rule.

Richard Wilson

Flag of the American Indian Movement

Also the Indian protestors were critical of the U.S. Government's failure to fulfil treaties with the First Nation People. They demanded that the treaty negotiations be reopened, and that fair and equitable treatment would result.

The protestors occupied the town for seventy-one days. They were surrounded by the United States Marshal Service and FBI agents and other law enforcement officers helped cordon off the town.

There were casualties on both sides; a U.S. Marshal was shot and was paralysed.

A Cherokee brave and an Oglala Indian were killed by gunshots from officers surrounding the town.

Civil rights activist Ray Robinson, a close associate of Martin Luther King entered the town to demonstrate his support for the Indians. He disappeared while in Wounded Knee and his body has never been found.

The Wounded Knee occupation attracted wide media attention including overseas.

Indians to Give Up Weapons Today

PINE RIDGE, S.D. (UPI) — Two key leaders of the occupation at Wounded Knee gave themselves up Monday and a government negotiator said the militants still in the historic hamlet will begin laying down their arms early today.

Carter Camp and Leonard Crow Dog, two leaders of American Indian Movement (AIM) members and sympathizers who have held the village by armed force for 70 days, emerged and were hurried off to Rapid City, S.D., to face criminal charges.

"The occupation is over—

cupiers for two hours, said there are "roughly 75 persons left in there." Government spokesmen estimated Sunday there were about 100 persons still in the hamlet.

"It is quite clear what the intention of the militants is: To seek to infiltrate through the lines prior to disarmament with their weaponry," the Justice Department spokesman said. "They may try burying other weapons."

Roubideaux said procedures for today's dispossession of arms were going smoothly. He said Crow Dog, known as the

The situation motivated many Native Americans and their supporters. Many travelled to Wounded Knee to join the protest.

59

The American public demonstrated their sympathy and support. It had become clear that there were widespread and long standing issues of injustice relating to the First Nation People.

After the protest ended two senior members of the AIM were indicted on charges relating to the protest. The Federal Court dismissed the charges. The Government appealed the decision but the appeal was dismissed.

Unfortunately not much was achieved by the protest.

Wilson was re-elected under a cloud of voter fraud and other abuses.

Violence became endemic on the reservation with political factions at each other's throats. Over the next three years after the protest Wilson's private militia the Guardians of the Oglala Nation killed more than sixty opponents including Pedro Bissonette, Director of the Oglala Sioux Civil Rights Organisation.

Despite this, Wounded Knee highlighted the problems facing American Indians and showed them they could have a voice which would be heard. Wounded Knee has become a symbol of First Nation activism.

April 3

The Mobile Phone Invented

Prior to 1973 mobile telephony was restricted to phones installed in cars and in the military.

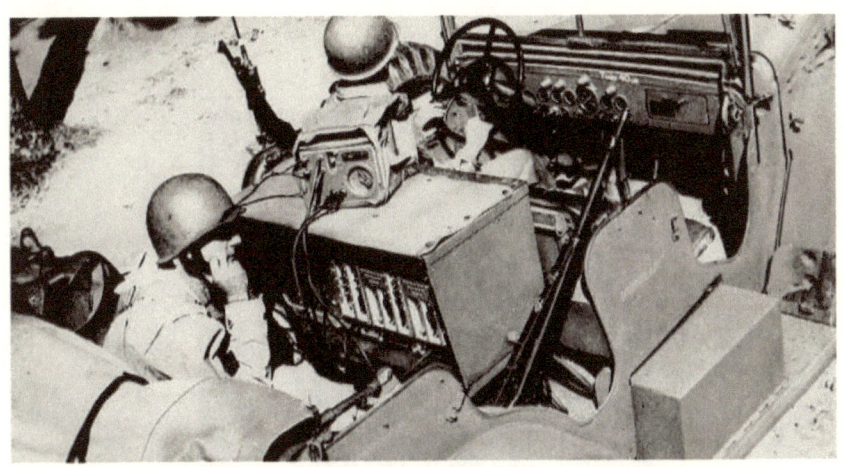

Motorola, a small technology company, invented the first handheld mobile phone.

On April 3, 1973, Motorola executive Martin Cooper made the first mobile phone call from a handheld phone to Dr Joel Engel of Bell Labs. Bell was also attempting to develop a mobile phone and Cooper's call was made to rub salt into the wound, proving that Engel had lost the race.

'Joel, I'm calling you from a cellular phone, a real cellular phone, a handheld, portable, real cellular phone,' Cooper said.

It wasn't said to be the most scintillating conversation, but it was historic, nonetheless. Mr Cooper kept the call very brief.

'I don't remember exactly what he said, but it was really quiet for a while. My assumption was that he was grinding his teeth. He was very polite and ended the call,' Cooper said of his rival.

The first mobile phone weighed 1.1 kilograms and measured 23cm X 13cm.

Talk time was limited to thirty minutes and it took ten hours to recharge. Motorola pursued the development of the technology and became a world leader in mobile phones.

Xiaomi (China) presently leads the global smartphone sales charts with a market share of 17.1 per cent in June 2021, followed by Samsung at second place with 15.7 per cent, and Apple at third place with 14.3 per cent.

March 8

The Northern Border Poll was a referendum held in Northern Ireland on 8 March 1973. The question was should Northern Ireland remain part of the United Kingdom or join the Republic of Ireland.
The result was conclusive
The voter turnout was 58.7% and 98.7% voted to remain in the United Kingdom.

The Old Bailey Bombing

The Old Bailey bombing was also known as Bloody Thursday in Britain.
The IRA detonated a car bomb outside the Old Bailey courthouse.
An eleven-person Active Service Unit from the Provisional IRA Belfast
Brigade carried out the attack.
The unit exploded another bomb outside Whitehall at the same time as
the Old Baily bomb.
This attack was the first major incident since the beginning of the
troubles in the 1960s.
Fortunately, only one person died though 220 were injured.
The perpetrators were all caught.

The Trial

The trial took place at Winchester Crown Court as the Old Bailey was
too badly damaged from the explosion.
The trial took ten weeks with William McLarnon pleading guilty on the
first day of the trial.

November 14 1973

The jury convicted six men and two women of the bombings. They acquitted Roisin McNearney in exchange for the information she gave the police, which helped bring about the convictions. She was given a new identity.

As the judge read her verdict out the other defendants began to hum the *Dead March from Saul*.

One of the six threw a coin at McNearney, shouting 'take your blood money with you'.

She left the court in tears.

The judge sentenced eight of the defendants to life imprisonment with an additional 20 years for conspiracy.

Nineteen-year-old William McLarnon was shown leniency with a 15-year sentence. When his sentence was announced, he yelled, 'Up the Provisional IRA.' The lifers raised their fists in defiance as they were taken down. Supporters and eventually the prisoners went on hunger strikes, demanding they serve their sentences on Irish soil. As part of a truce in 1975 they were transferred to a jail in Ireland.

The Death Toll During the Troubles

More than 3,500 people were killed in the conflict, of whom 52% were civilians, 32% were members of the British security forces and 16% were members of paramilitary groups. Republican paramilitaries (IRA) were responsible for some 60% of the deaths, loyalists 30% and security forces 10%.

9/11

The World Will Never Forget

World Trade Centre 1973

At the opening ceremony of the World Trade Centre on April 4, 1973, Minoru Yamasaki the Chief Architect made an ironic speech.

'The World Trade Centre is a living symbol of man's dedication to world peace... beyond the compelling need to make this a monument to world peace, the World Trade Centre should, because of its importance, become a representation of man's belief in humanity, his need for individual dignity, his belief in the cooperation of men. And through this cooperation his ability to find greatness.'

September 11

8.30

It was a beautiful morning, with not a cloud in the sky. The temperature was a mild 65 degrees.

John Bailey had just finished his shift as a Deputy Chief of the Manhattan Fire Brigade. There had not been any significant occurrences during his shift; only a couple of small fires.

He decided to call into his favourite coffee shop, the *Coffee Bean* and order a cappuccino and a French pastry.

He sat at the bar and, as he began to drink his coffee, he glanced up at the television.

8.46

What he saw shocked him. A passenger plane had just ploughed into the North Tower of The World Trade Centre.

What a terrible accident. I've got to get down there and see if I can be of assistance, he thought.

John's brother, a financial advisor, quite often ran courses using the facilities of *Windows on the World*, a restaurant on the 106th and 107th floors of the North Tower.

He hoped to God Geoff wasn't running a seminar that day. As he ran towards the Trade Centre precinct he tried calling Geoff at his office.

'Good morning, this is Bailey Financial Services, Amy speaking. Can I help you?'

'Amy it's John, Geoff's brother, can I speak with him please?'

'I'm sorry John, he's not here at the moment. Can I leave a message for him when he returns?'

'Amy this is very important. Can you tell me where Geoff is?'

'He's conducting a seminar at the World Trade Centre.'

'Oh my God.'

'What's wrong?'

'Turn on the TV in the boardroom. I'm sorry Amy. I've got to go.'

9.03

John was nearing the disaster site and he could clearly see the North Tower burning. He then saw a second American Airlines plane fly into the South Tower and explode.

This is no fucking accident this is a full-blown terrorism attack, he thought.

The first thing John did was to secure a set of powerful binoculars from a colleague onsite. He knew it was a long shot, but he trained the lenses on the 107th floor where he knew his brother would be.

He saw Geoff standing on the window ledge just before his beloved brother jumped.

Always the showman, Geoff swan-dived to meet his maker.

John was devastated yet he knew he must help save the others trapped in the Twin Towers.

Deputy Chief John Bailey

After twenty-four hours John went home exhausted, devastated and mourning for his younger brother. He at least had the support of a loving wife and two beautiful twin teenaged girls.

John had nightmares every night and he would wake up in a cold sweat. The nightmare was always the same; his brother jumping from the 107th floor of the North Tower.

He became very irritable, not only to his family but also his work mates. He took to drinking heavily and smoking dope. He was offered counselling but declined. After one year his marriage had broken up and he had been fired from the Fire Brigade. He lived in a small apartment in the Bronx and socialised with no one.

John had a classic case of PTSD but refused help. He was walking down the Grand Concourse when he heard the familiar sound of fire trucks with their sirens wailing. The first truck sped by him. John stepped in front of the second. He was killed instantly. The driver received extensive counselling. He suffered PTSD for the remainder of his life.

'It has become clear that the West in general and America in particular have an unspeakable hatred for Islam. ... It is the hatred of crusaders against America deserves to be praised because it was a response to injustice, aimed at forcing America to stop its support for Israel, which kills our people. ... We say that the end of the United States is imminent, whether Bin Laden or his followers are alive or dead, for the awakening of the Muslim nation has occurred. ... It is important to hit the economy (of the United States), which is the base of its military power...If the economy is hit they will become reoccupied.'
— Osama bin Laden

May 5

Led Zeppelin Tampa Stadium

Led Zeppelin broke a concert attendance record previously held by the Beatles at their Tampa Stadium performance in 1973 when 56,800 fans attended.

Tampa Stadium

April 8

"Drink to Me. Drink to My Health"
Pablo Picasso's last words

Born October 25, 1881, as Pablo Diego Jose Francisco de Paula Juan Nepomuceno Maria de los Remedios Cipriano
Died 8 April 1973

Pablo Picasso, Guernica, 1937. Oil on canvas.

May 14

Skylab

Skylab was the first U.S. space station launched into Earth orbit. Three successive crews of visiting astronauts carried out investigations of the human body's adaptation to the space environment, studied the sun in unprecedented detail, and undertook pioneering Earth-resources observations.

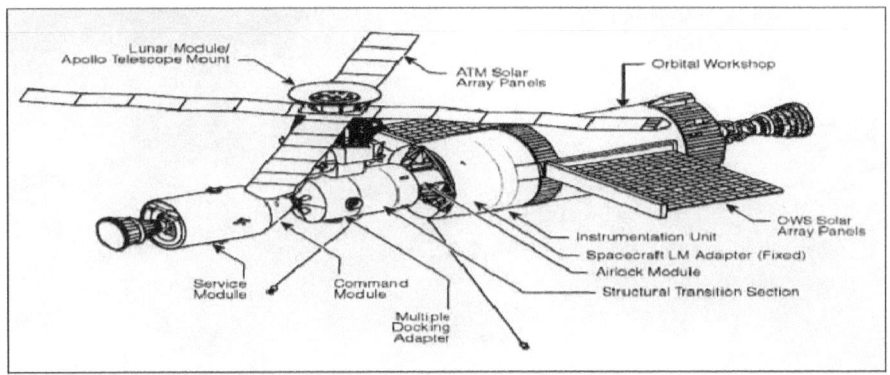

October 20

**The Opening of the Sydney Opera House
Opened by Queen Elizabeth 11**

Queen Elizabeth Opens the Opera House

December 31

AC/DC made their live debut when they appeared at Chequers Bar in Sydney.

1974

CHAPTER 5

Best Picture 1974

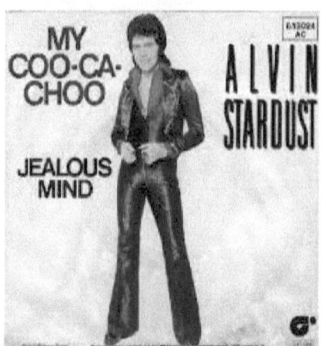

Number 1 Record 1975

I started the year by resigning from my accounting job and making an appointment with a personnel consultant from Drake International, reputably the largest personnel agency in the world. I hoped they would give me some vocational guidance.

I must have made an impression because the consultant referred me to his superior. He also was impressed and referred me to the State Manager of Drake Overload the temp division. After a lengthy interview he sent me to the Regional Manager. Paul Veith, the State Manager, needed Noel Wheeler's approval due to my age. I turned 22 on the 1ˢᵗ January and the minimum hiring age for Account Managers was 25.

They took a punt, and I was hired. I had two territories, Dandenong and Ringwood. These areas were twenty kilometres apart.

My accounting lecturer once suggested I would be better off in sales rather than accounting and he turned out to be right.

I continually topped the sales lists and was promoted to Brisbane Manager, becoming the youngest manager in the organisation. I had been with Drake for only six months.

My life in the sun had begun... or should I say my life in the heat and humidity.

Drake Paper Reporting My Appointment

January 20

The First F16 Flight

The YF-16, the aircraft that eventually led to the F-16 fighter, flew for the first time on January 20, 1974.

The flight was actually accidental, with the pilot taking off rather than crashing the plane.

The YF-16 prototype flew for six minutes before safely landing.

The F-16 Fighting Falcon fighter jet got off to a wobbly start. The prototype YF-16 jet nearly crashed during high-speed ground tests, an incident that could have killed the pilot and quite possibly the aircraft program itself. The pilot skilfully prevented disaster by taking the airplane into the air for an impromptu first flight—where it stayed for six minutes.

F16

Test Pilot Phil Oestricher

February 4

Patty Hearst was kidnapped outside her apartment in Berkeley California by the then unknown Symbionese Liberation Army.

Patty and fiancé, Steven Weed

Patty's townhouse, which she shared with Steven Weed

Around 9 p.m. there was a knock on the door of Patty Hearst's apartment. Steven Weed, Patty's fiancé, opened the door.

'Hands on your head and up against the wall you bourgeois bastard,' said Donald DeFreeze.

'Tie the prick's hands, Bob.'

'Where's the bitch?'

'I don't know who you are referring to.'

'Don't get smart with me. These guns are real and they're loaded. Cooperate and we may not shoot you. Now where is the Hearst bitch?'

Weed did not answer. Donald hit him with the butt of his rifle, creating a deep gash across his forehead.

'She's in the bedroom upstairs.'

'That's better. Keep an eye on him, Bob.'

The leader of the SLA climbed the stairs and entered the main bedroom. He could not see Patty. He looked under the bed but to no avail. He opened the sliding door of the wardrobe and discovered a petrified young woman.

'Patty Hearst I presume?'

'Don't hurt me, please. I'll do whatever you want.'

'Just put your hands out in front and you'll be fine.'

The SLA leader tied her hands and took her downstairs where she could see Steven sitting on the sofa with blood streaming down his face.

'Right, let's go.'

The terrorist group led Patty away. They placed her in the trunk of their car and drove off at great speed.

Patty's life would be changed forever.

The terrorists who kidnapped her called themselves the Symbionese Liberation Army, aka SLA.

A hardened criminal, Donald DeFreeze, led the group with the ambition to fight a guerrilla war against the United States Government. Their objective was to eliminate the capitalist state with the aid of black and white men and women, anarchists, extremists and other despots.

DeFreeze

The SLA had already shot two school officials, killing one and seriously wounding the other.

Why? Because the officials had mandated that students should carry identification cards.

What was the motivation to kidnap Patty Hearst?

DeFreeze knew that the entire country would be aware of the abduction. The Hearst family was renowned as a very powerful and wealthy family. Patty's grandfather was the newspaper magnate, William Randolph Hearst.

The plan worked. The kidnapping made front-page news around the country and was widely reported around the world.

The young heiress was taken to an SLA safe house in San Francisco and locked in a cupboard.

The house belonged to Bill and Emily Harris, members of the SLA.

The Harris Safe House

80

After a week in her improvised cell she was given some food. She couldn't eat it, which was probably a good thing as DeFreeze forbade her from leaving the cupboard to go to the bathroom.

'Patty, if you believe in God I'd be saying my prayers as you don't have long to live,' said DeFreeze. He was the only member of the SLA who was permitted to talk to her.

After a few more days DeFreeze demanded she make a tape recording, which he intended to release to the media.

'Mom, Dad, I'm with a combat unit that's armed with automatic weapons... I want to get out of here... and I just hope you'll do what they say.'

DeFreeze continued to threaten Patty with death although he did allow her out for meals. Her blindfold was removed, and she began to join in some political discussions.

She was given a flashlight, enabling her to read. What they gave her was SLA propaganda. She was expected to memorize these ramblings.

She was gradually being converted to the SLA philosophy. Finally, Patty was offered the choice to be released or to join the SLA.

She decided to stay and fight with the SLA.

'Well done Patty. Remove her blindfold and she can meet the group.'

This was the first time she had seen any of the members of the SLA other than DeFreeze.

From that point Patty was given daily lessons in weapon handling.

One of the key members of the SLA was Angela Atwood. She told Patti the group felt she should know about sexual freedom. William Wolfe and DeFreeze, it was alleged, raped Patti.

Patti Hearst made an audiotape to be released to the press announcing she had joined the SLA and taken the name Tania.

Angela Atwood School Photo

April 15

Tania, aka Patty Hearst, walked into the Sunset District branch of the Hibernia Bank in San Francisco wielding a M1 carbine.

She yelled, 'I'm Tania up, up, up against the wall you motherfuckers.'

The surveillance video camera recorded the scene.

Patty aka Tania in the bank

The FBI agent heading the investigation testified that SLA members were photographed pointing their guns at Hearst during the robbery.

A grand jury indicted her in June 1974 for the robbery.

Hearst remained an active member of the SLA until her capture. She committed several crimes including making bombs and kidnapping.

September 18

San Francisco police and FBI agents arrested Patty Hearst in a San Francisco apartment along with Wendy Yoshimura, a fellow SLA member.

Wendy Yoshimura

While she was being booked into jail, Hearst stated her occupation as "Urban Guerrilla".

She instructed her attorney to release this following message.

'I'm smiling and I feel strong, and I send my greetings and love to all the sisters and brothers out there.'

While being booked into jail, Hearst listed her occupation as "Urban Guerrilla" and asked her attorney to relay the following message: 'Tell everybody that I'm smiling, that I feel free and strong, and I send my greetings and love to all the sisters and brothers out there.'

Authorities noted that she had lost forty kilos during her capture and her IQ had dropped from 130 to 112; a significant reduction.

Psychiatrist Louis West who had been appointed by the court concluded she had been brainwashed. He later asked President Carter to release her.

Robert Lifton from Yale concluded that what Hearst suffered was similar to a prisoner of war.

March 20

Hearst was convicted of bank robbery and using a firearm during the felony. She was sentenced to 35 years in prison subject to a final sentence hearing. Her sentence was reduced to seven years.
Her time in prison was not an easy one; she suffered several medical problems including a collapsed lung.
Outside the walls, celebrities, including John Wayne, spoke in her defence.

February 1, 1979

President Jimmy Carter commuted Hearst's sentence and she was released under stringent conditions.

January 20, 2001

President Bill Clinton granted her a pardon on his last day in office.

Aftermath

Patti Hurst's estimated wealth is $50 Million
She has written several books and starred in a number of films.
She was married to Bernard Shaw in 1979. He died in 2013.
They had two children.

March 3

Turkish Airlines Flight 981

On the 3rd of March 1974, a packed Turkish Airlines DC-10 was rocked by a tremendous explosion shortly after take-off from Paris. A huge hole had opened up near the back of the cabin, throwing part of the floor, two rows of seats, and six passengers out into the sky. The pilots tried to save their crippled plane, but the pitch controls had been destroyed, sending the plane into an irrecoverable dive, and the jet crashed less than two minutes later in the Ermenonville Forest, killing all 346 passengers and crew.

The Crash Site

The Brady Bunch ran from September 26 until March 8 1974

I Love Lucy ran for 23 consecutive years.

I used to sneak into the lounge room thinking my parents couldn't see me. I hid under the sofa and watched I Love Lucy trying not to laugh. When the show finished I would sneak back into bed.

March 9

Hiroo Onoda

Hiroo was an Imperial Japanese Army Intelligence officer during World War II. He was unaware of Japan's surrender and spent 29 years hiding out in the Philippines. He was finally convinced of the war's end when his former commander travelled to the Philippines, relieving him from duty by order of the Emperor in 1974.

The last man standing was Teruo Nakamura who surrendered later in 1974.

April 6

ABBA wins the Eurovision Song Contest with their song *Waterloo*.

September 8

With much media fanfare, daredevil Evel Knievel tried and failed to leap the mile-wide chasm of the Snake River Canyon on his specially engineered rocket motorcycle.

October 30

Rumble in the Jungle

Muhammad Ali knocks out George Foreman in eight rounds to regain the heavyweight title, which had been stripped from him seven years earlier.

November 21

Birmingham Pub Bombings

Two pubs were bombed, killing 21 people in an attack believed to be linked to the IRA although the terrorist group never claimed responsibility.

Six men were arrested, tried and sentenced to life imprisonment. After a lengthy campaign by supporters their convictions were quashed and all six were released.

December 25

Darwin

Cyclone Tracy devastated Darwin in Australia's top end, ruining Christmas for some residents and killing 71 others.

Wind gusts reached 217 kilometres an hour before all the weather instruments failed. The anemometer at Darwin airport control tower had its needle bent in half by the gusts.

Tracy caused $837 million in damage (1974 dollars). That figure equates to $8 billion in today's terms.

More than 70% of Darwin was destroyed, leaving 25,000 residents homeless. Australia's largest evacuation was required; 30,000 people in all. Many would never return.

The city was rebuilt using very strict building standards.

Anemometer at Airport

THE DAY DARWIN DIED

1975

CHAPTER 6

Best Picture

Number 1 Record

I bought my first house in Paddington, Brisbane. I borrowed the deposit and the principal, leaving me in a fair amount of debt.

I paid $22,000 and spent all my spare time renovating it. My father helped when he could.

I sold it in 1980 for $40,000. Its most recent sale price was $1,400,000.

Charteris Street Paddington

I also got engaged to my first wife, Beth.

Riding trail bikes and surfing took second place to working on the house.

During my time with Drake I walked into the right company at the right time. It was a large building society that lost all their data when they went live on their IBM computer the same day there was a run on all the banks.

I eventually placed 100 temps for nine months to reconcile their accounts. Brisbane branch became the most profitable office in Drake International.

I didn't get acknowledgement from Bill Pollack the CEO and the $13,500 bonus would be spread over five years.

That bonus in today's terms would amount to $63,000.

I told them to shove it and accepted a sales role with TNT Payroll Management Systems in Sydney.

Yes, I was young and impetuous.

Other Significant Events in 1975

January

The President of Cambodia, Lon Nol, was overthrown when the Khmer Rouge led by Pol Pot occupied Phnom Penh. Prince Sihanouk became the head of state, albeit for a short time. Pol Pot renamed the country Kampuchea.

The regime forcibly removed all city dwellers to rural areas to work in forced labour camps.

Money became a worthless commodity; freedoms were removed, and all religion was banned.

Pol Pot coined the phrase "Year Zero".

Many thousands of the educated and middle classes were tortured and murdered in the killing fields.

Many thousands more died from disease or exhaustion.

Pol Pot sits in the same class as Hitler and Stalin, yet he was never prosecuted.

Pol Pot

January 18

Finally diplomatic relations between Bangladesh and Pakistan are established.

Watergate Scandal

John Mitchell. H.R. Haldeman and John Ehrlichman are found guilty of the Watergate cover-up.
They are sentenced to between 30 months and 8 years in prison.

January 5

Tasman Bridge Disaster

The Tasman Bridge disaster occurred on the evening of 5 January 1975, in Hobart a bulk ore carrier travelling up the Derwent River collided with two pylons of the Tasman Bridge, causing a large section of the bridge deck to collapse onto the ship and into the river below. Twelve people were killed, including seven crew on board the ship. Five occupants were killed in four cars, after driving off the bridge. Hobart was cut off from its eastern shore; residents relied on a ferry service to commute to the city. The ship's master was officially charged for inattention and failure to handle his vessel in a seamanlike manner.

Two Cars Had a Lucky Escape

February 11

One happy person; one not so happy

Margaret Thatcher defeated Edward Heath for the leadership Conservative Party of the United Kingdom. Thatcher became the first female leader of any political party in Britain.

March 4

Queen Elizabeth II knights Charlie Chaplin

April 4

Bill Gates and Paul Allen found Microsoft.

Microsoft staff 1975

Microsoft staff 1978

Microsoft Corp announced the following results for the quarter ended September 30, 2021, as compared to the corresponding period of last fiscal year: Revenue was $45.3 billion an increase of 22%. Operating income was $20.2 billion an increase of 27%.

April 30

The End of the Vietnam War

Finally the Vietnam War ends with the fall of Saigon.
South Vietnam surrenders unconditionally and is replaced with Provisional Government.

U.S. departure protocol

May 1

The Khmer Rouge raided several Vietnamese villages, slaughtering many villagers. This action leads to the Cambodian – Vietnamese War.

May 19

Elton John's "Captain Fantastic and the Brown Dirt Cowboy" becomes the first album to enter the U.S. Billboard 200 album chart at number one.

June 5

The Suez Canal opens for the first time since the Six-Day War in 1967.
On June 5, 1975, amid the echoes of a 21-gun salute, a seven-ship flotilla eased through ceremonial gates in mid-canal waters off Port Said and steamed south through the Suez Canal to Ismailia in a five-hour voyage marking the official reopening of the canal exactly eight years after its closure during the 1967 Arab-Israeli war.
For the maritime nations of the world, for the Middle East and, above all, for Egypt, it was an event of historic proportions. And if the ceremonies were less spectacular than those marking the original opening of the canal they were, nonetheless, impressive.

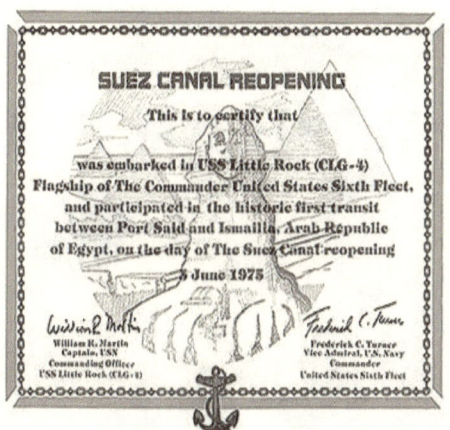

July 17

Apollo-Soyuz Test Project

A manned Apollo spacecraft and a manned Soviet Soyuz spacecraft dock in orbit, marking the first such link-up between spacecraft from the two nations.

October 1

The Thrilla in Manila—Muhammad Ali defeats Joe Frazier in a World Title fight.

October 16

Indonesia

The Balibo Five

The Balibo five was a group of journalists representing various Australian television networks covering the looming Indonesian invasion of East Timor.

The group comprised two Australians, reporter Greg Shackleton, 29, and sound man Tony Stewart, 21; a New Zealander, Gary Cunningham, 27, cameraman for the Seven Network and two Britons, cameraman Brian Peters, 24, and reporter Malcolm Rennie, 29, both working for the Nine Network.

They were all based in the town of Balibo in East Timor when they were killed on October 16 by Indonesian troops.

The Australian public were horrified, prompting an Australian journalist, Roger East to travel to Balibo to investigate what had happened.

He was murdered on the docks of the capital, Dili, by Indonesian troops.

The Australian Government has never objected to this murderous action by the Indonesian Government so as not to upset them.

November 11

The dismissal of the Whitlam government provided one of the biggest political shocks in Australian history. It put on display vice-regal powers that most did not know existed, and tested Australians' understanding of their own constitution and political system.

On October 16, 1975, the Senate resolved that it would not pass supply until the Whitlam government agreed to call a general election. This meant the Commonwealth would soon run out of money to pay public servants, provide pensions, pay its contractors, and provide services. The Whitlam government decided to tough it out in the hope the Coalition opposition would collapse.

Because the Christmas holidays were approaching, the last day to initiate a pre-Christmas election was November 13, 1975. If that deadline was missed, there would potentially be months of economic chaos with no money to run the government and pay salaries or pensions until February.

On the morning of November 11, Opposition Leader Malcolm Fraser told Gough Whitlam the Opposition would pass supply if Whitlam agreed to hold an election for both houses in May or June 1976. Whitlam refused.

Instead, Whitlam went to the Governor-General, Sir John Kerr, to seek a half-Senate election in December. This would not have been likely to resolve the impasse and would have been particularly problematic if supply was not granted to cover the election period.

When Whitlam declined to request a general election, Kerr exercised his reserve powers by dismissing Whitlam and his government from office. He then appointed Fraser as Prime Minister on the condition that he secured the passage of supply, advised the dissolution of both houses of parliament, and called an election in December.

Kerr also stipulated that Fraser's government must only be a caretaker government that would not make any major appointments or undertake any inquiries or investigations into the Whitlam government. The Senate passed the supply bills and once assent was given to them, both Houses were immediately dissolved.

It was then left to voters in the election to decide who should govern. The former Whitlam government was comprehensively defeated, and the Fraser government was elected to office in a landslide.

Sir John Kerr and Queen Elizabeth

December 7

Indonesia does what it has planned to do for some time, invade East Timor. The occupation continued until 1999 when the United Nations sent in peacekeepers to take control until 2002 when East Timor achieved independence.

Indonesian Troops in East Timor

Tanks Roll In

1976

CHAPTER 7

Best Picture 1976

Number One Record

January

My wife and I began our road trip to Sydney and a new life. I had just purchased my father's Toyota Crown Two Door, one of only six in Australia. He purchased it in London two years before. I paid the market price, $4,000.

A recent auction brought $1,100,000 for this car.

One of those, "I should never have sold it" moments.

It was a huge learning curve selling payroll bureau services to mostly large corporations.

The highlight of my time working in Sydney was selling Citicorp a payroll system; the most significant sale in the company's history.

I purchased a semi-detached in Woollahra for $44,000 and sold it 18 months later for $58,000. The 2021 valuation is $2,500,000. I was promoted to South Australian manager. So began three very enjoyable yet challenging years.

36 Adelaide Street Woollahra

Other Significant Events in 1976

January 5

The Khmer Rouge with Pol Pot as its leader proclaims a new constitution for democratic Kampuchea.
The genocide began.

January 21

From London's Heathrow Airport and Orly Airport outside Paris, the first Concordes with commercial passengers simultaneously take flight on January 21, 1976. The London flight was headed to Bahrain in the Persian Gulf, and Paris to Rio de Janeiro via Senegal in West Africa.

January 27

The U.S.A vetoes a United Nations resolution that called for an independent Palestinian state.
President Jimmie Carter was the newly elected President.

March

The first Cray supercomputer was installed at Los Alamos National Laboratory.
Cray eventually sold over 100 supercomputers around the world.

Cray Supercomputer

March

When Juan Perón died on July 1, 1974, his wife became president of a nation suffering from inflation, political violence, and labour unrest. In March 1976, she was deposed in an air-force-led coup, and a right-wing military junta took power. It brutally ruled Argentina until 1982.

Isabel Perón

March 27

Anita Roddick established a shop called The Body Shop, selling skin care and cosmetics in Brighton England.
There are now 3000 outlets around the world and turning over more than $4 Billion.

March 29

Jorge Videla becomes President of Argentina

In 1985, two years after the return of a democratic government, Videla was prosecuted for large-scale human rights and crimes against humanity that took place under his rule, including kidnappings, widespread torture and murder of activists and political opponents as well as their families at secret concentration camps. An estimated 13,000 to 30,000 political dissidents vanished during this period.

April 23

Too Old to Rock 'n' Roll: Too Young to Die! is the ninth studio album released by British band Jethro Tull, recorded in December 1975 and released in 1976.

April 1

Steve Jobs and Steve Wozniak form Apple Computer.

April 5

Hughes in the Cockpit of the Spruce Goose

Howard Hughes, billionaire businessman and aviator, dies.

Howard Hughes Jr. was a USA business magnate, investor, record-setting pilot, engineer, film director, and philanthropist, known during his lifetime as one of the most influential and financially successful individuals in the world.

He developed the world's largest plane constructed with wood. It got the nickname of "The Spruce Goose." It only flew once with Hughes at the controls.

Hughes became an eccentric

Howard Hughes invented an aerodynamic half-cup bra to support his budding leading lady Jane Russell in the movie The Outlaw. The bra supposedly allowed Jane to perform her action scenes without excessive bounce.

Jane Russell

May 6

The 1976 Friuli earthquake, also known in Italy as Terremoto del Friuli (Friulian earthquake), took place on May 6, 1976, with a moment magnitude of 6.5 and a maximum Mercalli intensity of X (Extreme). The shock occurred in the Friuli region in northeast Italy near the town of Gemona del Friuli.

The death toll was 900 and it left 100,000 homeless

April 1

Steve Jobs and Steve Wozniak debuted the Apple 1, a desktop computer that came as a single motherboard, pre-assembled, unlike other personal computers of that era. The Apple II was introduced about a year later.

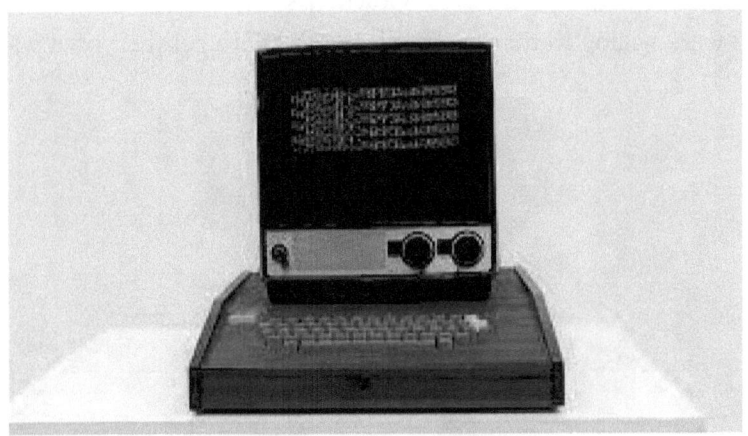

Apple 1 First Apple Computer

April 21
The Great Bookie Robbery

A well-organised crime gang of six stole what is widely believed to be $16 million (the 2021 equivalent would be $75 million).

The cash was stolen from the bookmakers from the Victoria Club located in central Melbourne, Australia.

The true figure for the amount stolen has never been confirmed, as the Victoria Club quoted the missing figure to police as only $1 million to avoid the attention of the Australian Tax Office (ATO). The gang included Raymond "Chuck" Bennett, who is believed to have been the mastermind, Ian Carroll, Laurence Prendergast and Norman Lee. They rented an office several floors above and hid the money in that room's safe before coolly walking out of the building and onto the street days after the event

The identity of the robbers was widely known in the underworld and so Bennett became the target of standover men, who included Brian and Leslie Kane, and corrupt police demanding part of the proceeds. The Kane brothers were particularly violent psychopaths who wanted their cut and were willing to torture, mutilate and kill to get their own way.

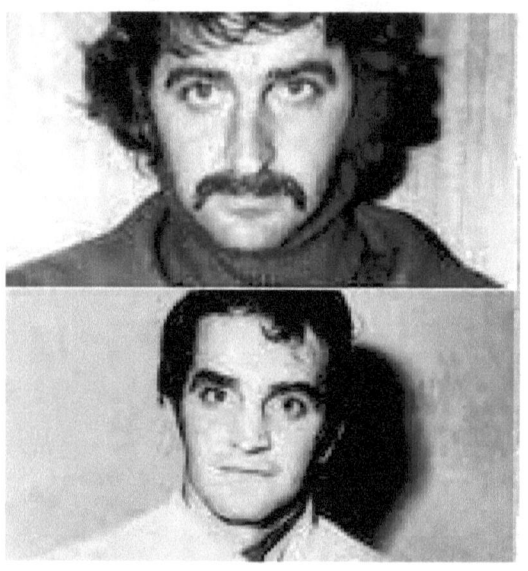

The Kane Brothers

After being told that the Kanes had intended to kill him, Bennett, Prendergast and Vincent Mikkleson murdered Leslie Kane on 19 October 1978 and went into hiding. The three were later arrested for the murder but as the body was never found, the charges were dismissed. With Brian Kane threatening to kill him, Bennett was arrested on a minor charge in 1979. While being escorted by police from the courthouse holding cells to the courtroom, he was taken up a flight of stairs into the path of a man disguised as a barrister. The man shot Bennett several times in the chest. Bennett tried to flee but collapsed on the courthouse steps and died a short time later. Although Brian Kane was suspected, circumstantial evidence suggested a conspiracy to kill Bennett, which included senior members of the Victorian Police, most notably Brian Murphy with whom Bennett had a long-standing feud.

Brian Murphy

No one has ever been arrested for Bennett's murder, which was, in effect, an execution. The money was never recovered and although Norman Lee was charged, he was later acquitted. None of the other members of the gang was ever convicted. Prendergast disappeared in 1985, and apart from Lee, the rest of the gang had all been murdered by the end of 1987. In 1992, Lee was killed by police during a heist at Melbourne. Lee's lawyer, Phillip Dunn, QC, later revealed the details of the crime, including the identities of all those involved. As no one was ever jailed or convicted, the Great Bookie robbery technically remains an unsolved crime.

July 3-4

Entebbe Raid
Uganda

The Entebbe raid was a rescue by an Israeli commando squad of 103 hostages from a French jet airliner hijacked en route from Israel to France. After stopping at Athens, the airliner was hijacked on June 27 by members of the Popular Front for the Liberation of Palestine and the Red Army Faction, (a West German radical leftist group) and flown to Entebbe Uganda, where additional accomplices joined them. At Entebbe, the hijackers freed those of the 258 passengers who did not appear to be Israeli or Jewish and held the rest hostage for the release of 53 militants imprisoned in Israel, Kenya and West Germany and elsewhere. In response, Israel on July 3 dispatched four Hercules C-130H cargo planes carrying 100–200 soldiers and escorted by Phantom jet fighters. After flying some 4,000 km from Israel to Uganda, the Israeli force rescued the hostages within an hour of landing. All seven of the militants were killed, and 11 MiG fighters supplied to Uganda by the Soviet Union were destroyed; the Israelis lost one soldier and three hostages during the operation. On the return trip, the Israeli planes met an awaiting hospital plane and refuelled at Nairobi Kenya. The success of the Entebbe raid substantially boosted Israeli morale.

The Israeli Rescue Team

July 17

Nadia Comaneci – The perfect 10

Before the 1976 Montreal Olympics, the Games' timekeepers Omega asked the IOC if they needed a new scoreboard to display a score of a perfect 10, as extra space was required to show 10.00. But the IOC refused, saying a perfect score was not possible.

Romanian gymnast Nadia Comaneci, aged just 14, took part in the team compulsory portion.

Her routine on the uneven bars was simply flawless. The judges awarded her full marks but since the scoreboard couldn't accommodate the digits, 1.00 was flashed on the screen.

It took some time for everyone to realise that history had been created as Comaneci was given a standing ovation.

July 20

NASA's Viking Project found a place in history when it became the first U.S. mission to land a spacecraft safely on the surface of Mars and return images of the surface. Two identical spacecraft, each consisting of a lander and an orbiter, were built. Each orbiter-lander pair flew together and entered Mars orbit; the landers then separated and descended to the planet's surface.

The Viking 1 lander touched down on the western slope of Chryse Planitia (the Plains of Gold), while the Viking 2 lander settled down at Utopia Planitia.

July 29

New York City

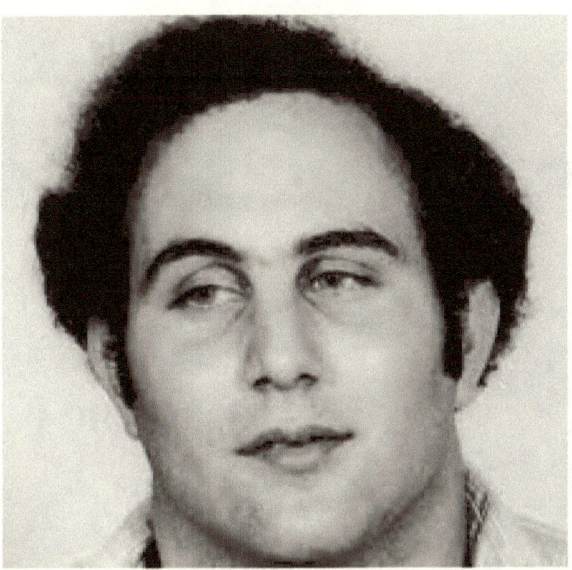

The Son of Sam pulled a gun from a paper bag and pulled the trigger killing one and seriously wounding another. This murder was the first in a series of murders that terrorised the city for the next year.

July 15

Bruce Jenner, later to become Caitlyn Jenner, wins the gold medal in the men's decathlon in the Montreal Olympics.

August 1

Niki Lauda, defending world F1 champion, suffered extreme burns after crashing in the 1976 German Grand Prix. He was lucky to survive.

September 9

Mao Dies

Mao Zedong was Chairman of the Chinese Communist Party from 1943 until his death.

Mao Zedong and his government was responsible for vast numbers of deaths with estimates ranging from 40 to 80 million victims through starvation, persecution, prison labour, and mass executions.

September 25

Irish rock group U2 was formed after drummer Larry Mullen posted a note on the school notice board seeking musicians to form a band in Dublin.

They chose the name after the U.S spy plane.

U2 Spy Plane

U2 Rock Group

November 2

Jimmy Carter wins the U.S. presidential election defeating the incumbent Gerald Ford.

1977

CHAPTER 8

This was the year I began my overseas travels. Naturally it began in Bali and Yogyakarta. Yes I've been to Bali too, although before most Australians.

The highlight of the trip was climbing Borobudur in central Java, a magnificent Buddhist temple. Having also been to Angkor Wat I would have to say the later was the more impressive, but nevertheless Borobudur was incredible.

Borobudur

Through work and leisure I have travelled overseas more than forty times. Why? You'll have to wait for the sequel.

Other Significant Events in 1977

January 3

Apple Computer is incorporated.
Apple II released in the same year.

January 17

Gary Gilmore is executed by firing squad in Utah. Gilmore had insisted he be executed for the two murders he admitted to committing. He was the first person executed in the United States in ten years.

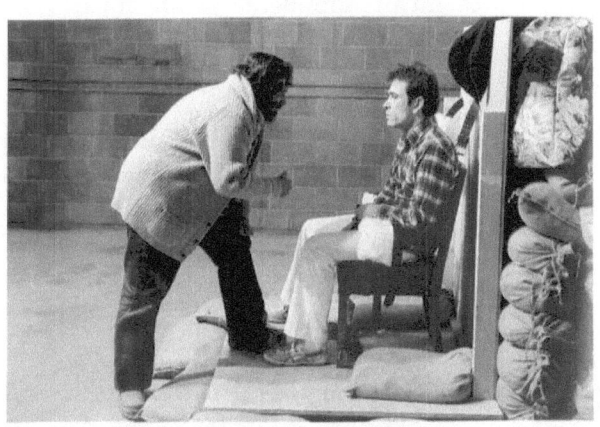

Gilmore's last words were "Let's Do It."

January 18

Scientists identify a previously unknown bacterium as the cause of Legionnaire's Disease.
Legionella was discovered after an outbreak in 1976 among people who

went to a Philadelphia convention of the American Legion. Those who were affected suffered from a type of pneumonia that eventually became known as Legionnaires' disease.

January 18

Granville Railway Disaster
Sydney, Australia

A commuter train brought predominately white-collar workers into the Sydney CBD to begin what they all thought would be a normal day.

The train derailed, running into the supports of a road bridge that collapsed onto two of the train's passenger carriages. The official enquiry found the primary cause of the crash to be poor fastening of the track.

It remains the worst rail disaster in Australian history: 83 people died, more than 213 were injured, and 1,300 were affected.

January 19

U.S. President Gerald Ford on his final day in office pardoned Tokyo Rose.

Iva Ikuko Toguri D'Aquino, aka Tokyo Rose was an American who participated in English-language radio broadcasts transmitted by Radio

Tokyo to Allied soldiers in the South Pacific during World War II on The Zero Hour radio show.

Jimmy Carter was sworn in as the 39th President of the United States.

January 21

President Carter pardons Vietnam War draft evaders.

February 4

Rumours is the eleventh studio album by British-American rock band Fleetwood Mac.

Sells 40 million copies

February 18

First flight of the space shuttle Enterprise mated to a Boeing 747

March 27

Tenerife Airport Spain

Two Boeing 747 passenger aircraft, a KLM Flight and a Pan Am Flight collided on the runway in Tenerife Spain. Resulting in 583 fatalities, the Tenerife airport disaster is the deadliest in aviation history.

A terrorist incident at Gran Canaria Airport had caused many flights to be diverted to Los Rodeos, including the two aircraft involved in the accident. The airport quickly became congested with parked airplanes blocking the only taxiway and forcing departing aircraft to taxi on the runway instead. Patches of thick fog were drifting across the airfield; hence visibility was greatly reduced for pilots and the control tower had limited visibility.

The collision occurred when the KLM airliner initiated its take-off run while the Pan Am airliner, shrouded in fog, was still on the runway and about to turn off onto the taxiway. The impact and resulting fire killed everyone on board KLM 4805 and most of the occupants of Pan Am 1736, with only 61 survivors in the front section of the aircraft.

Two Planes Colliding

June 26

Elvis Presley held his last concert at Market Square Arena in Indianapolis U.S.A.

August 16

Elvis dies

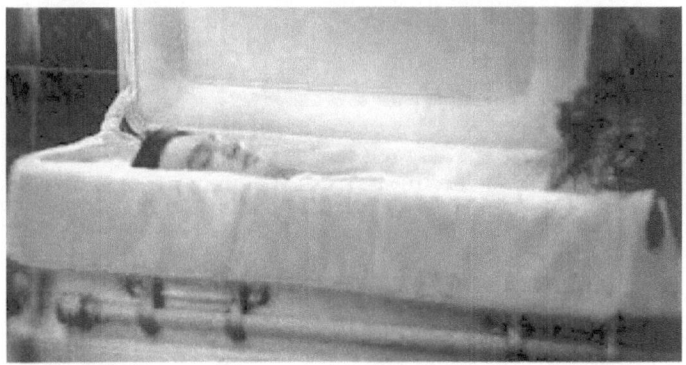

My family had a holiday house on Phillip Island Victoria. Whenever a new Elvis movie came out my friends and I would go to the Cowes flicks to watch him do his stuff.

We saw
Flaming Star
G.I. Blues
Blue Hawaii
And finally Wild in the Country

July 10

Greece suffers from an intensive heat wave and the temperature rises to a record 48 degrees Celsius.

Trying to Cool Down

July 13

New York Blackout

New York is without power for 25 hours. Looting is rampant and the Big Apple's citizens are in fear knowing Son of Sam was out there.

Looting in New York

July 22

The purged Chinese communist leader Deng Xiaoping was restored to power nine months after the "Gang of Four" was expelled from power in a coup d'état.

Gang of Four

In a career often described as "winding," Deng lived through war and revolution, exhilarating political triumphs and personal achievements, and equally humiliating downfalls and family tragedies. The tenacious Deng managed to not only endure all this, but to prevail.

Deng was also referred to as "The last Emperor" of China, a title one of his four daughters said he would never embrace, as he always maintained a strong disdain for the cult of personality.

Deng Rong said her father's primary wish in life was "to live the life of a genuine ordinary citizen, or even simpler than the way most people live." This, from the man who for nearly two decades held the destiny of at least one-quarter of humanity in his hands.

August 3

Tandy released a personal computer; the TRS 80 Model 1.
The memory of the TRS 80 started at 4kb and could be expanded to 48kb; it used a cassette player as its disc drive.
Over 100,000 units were sold in the 70s.

When I moved to Sydney to join TNT Payroll Systems we trialled the TRS80 to determine if we could sell a package of software and the TRS80. It was decided it was too slow to run a small payroll.

August 10

David Berkowitz was captured in Yonkers New York after a year of terror and eight senseless murders.

Berkowitz is alive and living in Shawangunk Prison. He is now 67 years old (2021)

August 19

A comedy legend dies. Grouch Marx died of pneumonia in Los Angeles at the age of 86.

Julius Henry "Groucho" Marx was an American comedian, actor, writer, stage, film, radio, and television star. He was generally considered to have been a master of quick wit and one of America's greatest comedians.

He made thirteen feature films as a team with his siblings, the Marx Brothers, of whom he was the third-born. He also had a successful solo career, primarily on radio and television, most notably as the host of the game show *You Bet Your Life*.

Young Groucho

Old Groucho

I remember as a boy of ten being home alone sick. I watched *Duck Soup* and fell into uncontrollable laughter. I'm sure I have never laughed so much watching a film since, although maybe *Life of Brian* is a contender.

The Marx Brothers

September 12

South African activist Steve Biko died after suffering a massive head injury while in police custody in Pretoria.

September 18

America's Cup Challenge
Newport, Rhode Island

The US defender, *Courageous*, skippered by Ted Turner, defeated the Australian challenger, *Australia*, skippered by Noel Robins, in a four-race sweep. Courageous' greatest winning margin out of all four races was 2 minutes and 23 seconds.

The America's Cup

October 21

British Punk Band the Sex Pistols released *Never Mind the Bollocks Here's the Sex Pistols* on the Virgin Record label.

Because of the profanity, most record retailers refused to stock it. What the fuck; it entered the charts at number one a week after its release.

The alternative

Hard Rock Cafe

Carole King

1977

 LYRICS
MUSICLYPZ

November 10

The soundtrack of *Saturday Night Fever* is released. The music was written and sung by the Bee Gees, and it became the best-selling album of all time up until 1977.

The album sold 40 million copies.

Thriller by Michael Jackson overtook the Bee Gees in 1982. It sold 70 million records.

November 19

The Egyptian President became the first Arab leader to make an official visit to Israel. He met with the Israeli Prime Minister Menachem Begin to negotiate a permanent peace settlement.

1978

CHAPTER 9

Best Picture

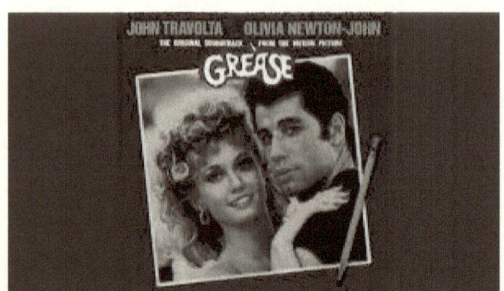

No 1 Record

I sold my beloved Toyota Crown, as I needed to justify my car allowance. I purchased a BMW 2800.

It was a beautiful car to drive but when driving from Adelaide to the Gold Coast to spend Christmas with the family a front tyre delaminated doing 160 kilometres an hour. We were very lucky to survive that mishap. I felt unsure of the BMW after that incident, so I bought an Alfa Romeo.

My life was pretty uneventful in 1978 apart from flying from Adelaide to Darwin twice in the TNT Lear Jet.

I hitched a ride to develop the bureau market up north.

I was able to sign up several accounts, but the highlight happened in the Darwin Hotel. I ordered a steak and decided a nice bottle of red would be nice. On the wine list was a Grange Hermitage 1970 for $15. I couldn't believe it. I was enjoying my meal and drinking the Grange when the publican approached me.

'Do you like the wine sir?'

'Yes. I do. It's magnificent.'

'People don't drink red wine up here; they prefer white or beer. Would you be interested in buying my remaining stock?'

'That depends how many bottles you have.'

'Twenty-four.'

'How much?'

'I'd have to charge $7 a bottle.'

'Okay, I'll take them.'

In 2021 a bottle of a 1970 Grange Hermitage goes for $1300.
It took me six years to drink them all although I did give one or two to my parents.

Concerts attended were:
The Beach Boys
Bob Dylan
David Bowie

Other Significant Events in 1978

January 6

The Holy Crown of Hungary was returned to Hungary from the United States where it had been held since World War II. It was given to the U.S. for safekeeping. Hungary feared the USSR would steal it.

The Holy Crown of Hungary, also known as the Crown of Saint Stephen, was the coronation crown used by the Kingdom of Hungary for most of its existence; kings have been crowned with it since the twelfth century.

February 9

Serial killer Ted Bundy was arrested; this sadistic sociopath admitted to thirty murders but police believe it could have been many more.
He was executed by electric chair on January 24, 1989.

February 1

Roman Polanski, the renowned film director, skipped bail and absconded to France after pleading guilty to charges of engaging in sex with a 13-year-old girl.

Polanski continued to direct films from his safe haven in France.

Notable films included *Tess, The Pianist, The Ghost Writer, Venus in Fur* and *An Officer and a Spy*. He received several awards including an Academy Award for Best Director for *The Pianist*. He didn't collect them personally!

February 13

The Sydney Hilton Hotel Bombing

The bomb was placed in a garbage bin outside the Hilton Hotel.

A garbage truck collected it, which triggered the bomb. Two City Council workers and a policeman were killed instantly, and another seven people were seriously wounded.

The Australian Prime Minister Malcolm Fraser and eleven heads of state were staying at the hotel. They were all attending a Commonwealth Heads of Government Meeting.

Ananda Marga, a religious terrorist group, was blamed. It was thought the bomb was targeting the Indian Prime Minister, Morarji Desai.

Several members of Ananda Marga were arrested, tried and jailed. They were later released.

Carnage in a Sydney Street

February 16

Hillside Stranglers Arrested

Two related (cousins) serial killers terrorised Los Angeles between October 1977 and February 1978.

Many of the victims were discovered in the hills above L.A.

Police finally identified the killers as Kenneth Bianchi and Angelo Buono.

They were tried and convicted of kidnapping, rape, torture and murder.

They were both convicted and sentenced to life imprisonment without parole.

February 21

I Think We Found a Pyramid
Mexico City

Two electrical workers were digging on a construction site at a location called Island of the Dogs, so called because dogs would congregate on the elevated position when flooding occurred.

'Hey Carlos, come and have a look at this.'

'Look at what?'

'Just come and take a look.'

'It looks like a bloody big rock to me. What's the big deal?'

'You're not looking close enough. We need to scrape the clay off it.'

'Okay, you scrape, and I'll supervise.'

'You're fucking hopeless, Carlos.'

'Enough of the insults and start scraping.'

As Juan began scraping the clay from the so-called rock, carvings began to appear.

'Carlos, I told you it was more than a rock. By the look of the carving I think it could be Inca.'

'I think you might be right, Juan; we better let the boss know.'

When the foreman arrived at the site an hour later, he concluded the stone was an Inca artefact of some sort although he was no archaeological expert. He contacted The Instituto Nacional de Antropología e Historia, the Government department responsible for all historical sites.

What Juan and Carlos had discovered was a pre-Hispanic monolith. This stone turned out to be a huge disc of over 3.25 metres in diameter, 30 centimetres thick and weighing 8.5 metric tons. The relief on the stone was later determined to be Coyolxauhqui, Huitzilopochtli's sister, and was dated to the end of the 15th century.

From 1978 to 1982, specialists, directed by archaeologist Eduardo Matos Moctezuma, worked on the project to excavate the Temple. Initial excavations found that many of the artefacts were in good enough condition to study. Efforts coalesced into the Temple Mayor Project, which was authorised by presidential decree.

To excavate, thirteen buildings in the area had to be demolished. Nine of these were built in the 1930s, and four dated from the 19th century, and had preserved colonial elements. During excavations, more than 7,000 objects were found, mostly offerings including effigies, clay pots in the image of Tlaloc, skeletons of turtles, frogs, crocodiles, and fish; snail shells, coral, some gold, alabaster figurines, ceramic urns, decorated skulls and knives.

Temple Mayor

The above image depicts the temple, as it was in the 15th century.

The Archaeological Site Present Day

March 9

Terror
Coastal Highway near Tel Aviv

Thirteen Palestinian terrorists departed from Lebanon on a mission of terror against their hated enemy Israel. They all belonged to Palestinian Fedayeen from Fatah.

They made their way in a large powerboat, transferring to two Zodiacs, and headed for the Israeli shore. Their weapons included Kalashnikov rifles, rocket propelled grenades, mortars and high explosives.

Kalashnikov Rifle

The sea was rough. Waves broke over the Zodiacs and two of the terrorists were washed overboard and drowned.

The eleven survivors landed on a beach near a kibbutz.

Gail Rubin was a professional photographer staying at the kibbutz; she was taking nature photos for a well-known magazine on the beach when the Palestinians approached her.

'Excuse me, miss we seem to be lost. Could you tell us where we are?' asked the only female in the group, Dalal Mughrabi.

'Yes, certainly. You are close to Maagan Kibbutz which is not far from the coastal highway.'

'Thank you.'

Maagan then shot several bullets into the American's chest. She died instantly. The Coastal Road Massacre had begun.

The group followed Gail's directions and headed for the four-lane highway. When they reached the highway they began shooting at the passing traffic. They hijacked a taxi, shooting its passengers and driver first. They all crammed in and headed for Tel Aviv. They noticed a bus parked at a bus stop, and they hijacked the bus and all its passengers. It was a company bus, and the passengers were bus drivers and their families.

They continued their journey to Tel Aviv, throwing grenades at passing cars and shooting their rifles. One passenger was thrown out of the speeding bus.

Police set up roadblocks and a fire fight ensued. It all ended when the bus erupted in a ball of flames.

A total of 38 civilians were killed in the attack including 13 children. There were 71 wounded and of the 11 remaining terrorists 9 were killed.

The two surviving perpetrators, Khaled Abu Asba and Hussein Fayyad, were arrested and tried in an Israeli military court in Lod.

On 23 October 1979, they were convicted on all 13 charges. They were sentenced to life imprisonment and spent seven years in prison before being released in the 1985 Jibril Agreement (prisoner exchange).

Israeli Reprisal

The 1978 South Lebanon conflict was an invasion by Israel of southern Lebanon up to the Litani River in March 1978 in response to the Coastal Road massacre. The conflict resulted in the deaths of 1,100–2,000

Lebanese and Palestinians, 20 Israelis, and the internal displacement of 100,000 to 250,000 people in Lebanon.

March 16

Red Brigade terrorists kidnapped Aldo Moro, former Italian Prime Minister. Five of his bodyguards were killed defending their leader.

Moro while Being Held in Captivity

May 9

Moro's bullet riddled body was discovered in the centre of Rome close to the Coliseum. He was in the back of a Renault 4.

There have been many conspiracy theories surrounding Moro's kidnapping and murder.
The CIA, Henry Kissinger and the Mafia are but a few.
The Red Brigade members were captured, tried and imprisoned.

Name	Date of capture	Outcome
Corrado Akunni	1978	Semi-freed in 1997
Marina Zoni	1978	
Valerio Morucci	1979	Life imprisonment; freed in 1994 due to his dissociation
Barbara Balzerani	1985	Life imprisonment; paroled in 2006
Marion Moretti	1981	6 life imprisonments; semi-freed in 1997
Alvaro Lojacono	Never	Fled to Switzerland
Allesio Casimirri	Never	Fled to Nicaragua, where he currently owns a restaurant

Rita Algranati	2004	Captured in Cairo; life imprisonment
Adriana Faranda	1979	Freed in 1994 due to her collaboration
Prospero Gallinari	1979	Life imprisonment; home detention from 1996. Gallinari died in 2013

June 12

Serial killer David Berkowitz aka Son of Sam is sentenced to 365 years in prison. Chances are he'll die there.

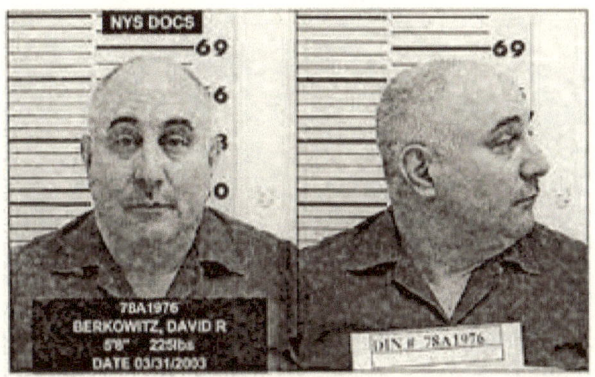

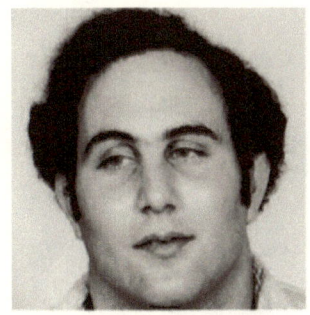

David has aged a little in prison.
I am also the Son of Sam. Sam was my much-loved father.

June 19

Garfield the cat is launched across several U.S. based newspapers. Garfield becomes the most popular syndicated comic strip ever.

July 25

Louise Brown was the first human to be born through IVF. Her birth through the system pioneered in Britain has been lauded among the most remarkable medical breakthroughs of the 20th century.

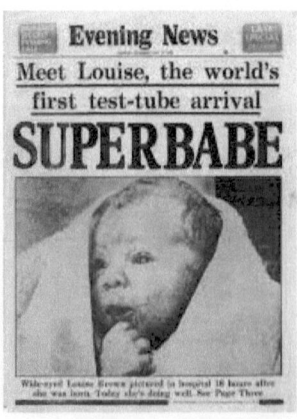

Louise and her family

September 7

Keith Moon, drummer of the WHO, died from an overdose at the age of 32. He was regarded as one of the best drummers of his era.

September 17

Peace in the Middle East an oxymoron?

Egyptian President Anwar Sadat and the Israeli Prime Minister Menachem Begin signed the Camp David Accords. The two adversaries had been secretly negotiating for twelve days at Camp David in Maryland U.S.A.

Camp David

The agreements were signed at the White House. The then President Jimmie Carter witnessed the signatures.
These agreements led to the 1979 Egypt - Israel Peace Treaty.
The 1978 Nobel Peace Prize was awarded jointly to Sadat and Begin.

Sadat and Begin Receive the Peace Prize

September 7

Georgi Markov

Georgi Markov was born in Bulgaria. He loved his country but despised Bulgaria's corrupt Prime Minister and his corrupt government. After great contemplation he decided to defect to Great Britain.

Georgi was regarded as a very good journalist. He joined the BBC and wrote for a number of other newspapers and journals.

He was critical of Todor Zhivkov, the Bulgarian PM and criticised him in various articles and broadcasts. He presented a radio program on Radio Free Europe, which cast aspersions on Russia and Bulgaria.

Zhivkov had had enough. He sought the help of the KGB to assassinate Markov.

Poisons were a preferred method to eliminate dissidents.

The KGB designed and manufactured the umbrella which would shoot and inject the microscopic sphere into Markov's thigh.

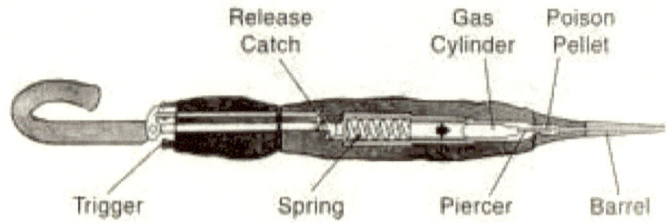

It is believed the poison used was ricin.

Georgi stood on London Bridge waiting for a bus to take him to the BBC studios.

He took very little notice of the man with the umbrella. Suddenly he felt a sharp pain on the back of his thigh. Georgi turned around to see the man with the umbrella. He apologised to Georgi and jumped in a taxi.

Georgi boarded the bus and went to work. Four days later he was dead. Nobody has ever been charged with the murder.

28 September

Pope John Paul died after only 33 days in office.
He was the first pope born in the 20th century and the last one to die in the 20th century. His reign was among the shortest in Papal history.

December 31, 1964

The young man watched Donald Campbell speed across Lake Eyre in South Australia on his Ferris 17-inch television. Campbell broke the water speed record that day. He reached 444.71 kilometres an hour.

Blue Bird

Ken Warby had followed Donald Campbell's career since he read about the Englishman's water speed record of 325.60 km/h in 1955. Ken was just 16 at the time.

'Hey, Dad, I'm going to break his record one day.'

'How do you propose to do that, son? It will take a lot of money and a lot of courage to go that fast across water.'

'You wait. I'll do it.'

'I wish you well Ken; let me know if you need a hand building the boat.'

Ken left school and worked at various jobs until eventually he landed a position as the Makita salesman for Newcastle and the Hunter Valley.

He now had access to the tools he needed to construct his dream.

Every spare moment Ken sketched designs for what would be the fasted boat on Earth. He decided on one particular design.

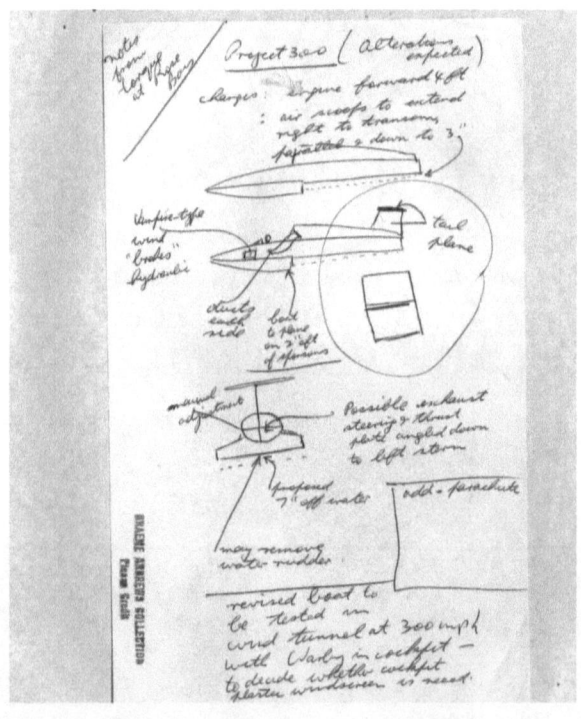

1972

Ken began the task of building the world's fastest speedboat. His work shed was his backyard, which meant he could work only in fine weather. The other restriction was he could work only in daylight. Materials such as plywood would be purchased when his limited budget would allow. Despite working for Makita, the only power tools he had at his disposal were a circular saw, a drill and a belt sander. He used hand tools for a significant amount of the construction.

During January 1973, a friend introduced Warby to two Leading Aircraft Men.

'I suppose you don't have a couple of jet engines lying around do you, Geoff?'

'No, I'm sorry Ken, but the Air Force has an auction every April. You never know your luck, mate.'

'Well, I think we should give it a go. Bring John with you; he's got an eye for a bargain.'

The three men, Warby, Crandall and Cox, attended the auction. They couldn't believe their luck! There were three Westinghouse jet engines up for auction.

There were no other bidders and they picked up the three for $265.

Crandall and Cox refurbished them and helped Ken fit one onto the boat.

Spirit of Australia Outside Ken's Home

1974

The *Spirit of Australia* was complete and ready to go and break some records.

On 20 November 1977, Ken set a new world water speed record of 464.46 km/h, breaking the record of Lee Taylor by a little over 4.8 km/h.

1978

With a subsequent 511.1 km/h run on 8 October 1978, he set the record that still stands today.

In doing so, he became the first and only person to exceed 482.8 km/h on water and live to tell the tale; Donald Campbell died on his attempt after his hydroplane crashed at over 515 km/h on his return run in his 1967 record attempt.

Warby After Breaking Speed Record

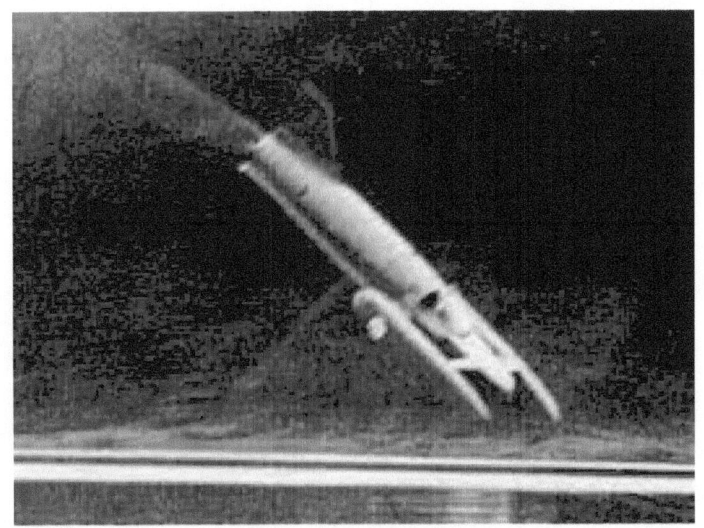

Campbell's Bluebird Demise

November 19

Jonestown Massacre
Guyana

The story of Jonestown begins with Jones, a white minister who preached unconventional progressive ideas to a congregation called the People's Temple. At the height of its popularity during the 1970s, the temple had a membership estimated in the thousands and was supported by many influential politicians. However, by 1977, Jones had grown paranoid from the media scrutiny over the temple's suspicious activities, so he and his numerous followers moved from San Francisco to an agricultural settlement in Guyana.

Jim Jones

Congressman Leo Ryan was concerned about the welfare of the Jonestown inhabitants, and he decided to fly down to Jonestown and see for himself. He arrived on November 14. He was given a tour of the settlement and was approaching his charter plane when gunmen opened fire, killing the Congressman and four of his party.

Following the murders, Jones commanded his followers to drink cyanide-laced punch, starting with the children first. In all, there were over nine hundred who died in Jonestown, including Jim Jones, who was found with a bullet to the head. It was assumed he had committed suicide.

900 suicided

1979

CHAPTER 10

Best Picture

Number 1 Record

My time in Adelaide ended when we decided to travel to Europe and work in Britain for a few years. I wrote to several I.T. companies in the U.K. and received a reply from the largest application software company in the world; Management Science America aka MSA.

The only issue was that the reply came from MSA Australia based in Sydney. After a couple of interviews I was offered and accepted a Sales Executive position. My area was South Australia and Western Australia and after six months I was given Victoria and Queensland. You can imagine the amount of travel involved. I was on a $60,000 package, which was a significant amount of money in those days.

MSA transferred me back to Sydney, and our little semi in Woollahra was now valued at $140,000.

After six months living back in Sydney I learned my father had cancer. I resigned from the company and intended to move up to Brisbane so we could support my mum and dad. Judith Lightfoot, the Managing Director, refused my resignation and instead allowed me to work from home in Brisbane. A magnificent woman.

My father died on 24th March 1982. I still miss him.

January 9

The Music for UNICEF Concert:

February 1

The+

Persian Empire Ends

A chartered Air France flight from Paris touched down at Mehrabad International Airport near central Tehran, carrying Iran's most revered spiritual figure.

Ayatollah Khomeini, an outspoken critic of Iran's ruler the Shah of Iran, was coming home after fourteen years in exile in Turkey, Iraq and France.

Before landing, the plane circled low overhead, reportedly to make sure that no tanks were blocking the runway.

Wearing his trademark black robe and turban, the 78-year-old cleric slowly emerged from the aircraft holding onto the pilot with his right hand. His son, Ahmad, followed closely.

Reports say between five to 10 million people showed up for his arrival, coming just days after the Shah abandoned his throne. He fled his then-tumultuous country, leaving the Iran-US alliance in tatters. The revolution would end the 2,500-year-old Persian Empire.

The Shah of Iran

February 3

Ayatollah Khomeini created the Council of the Islamic Revolution.

February 7

Supporters of Ayatollah Khomeini take over the Iranian law enforcement, courts and government administration; the final session of the Iranian National Consultative Assembly is held.

February 10

The Iranian army withdraws to its barracks, leaving power in the hands of Ayatollah Khomeini and ending the Pahlavi dynasty.

February 17

China invaded its neighbour to force Vietnam to withdraw from its very good ally Cambodia.

Chinese crossing into Vietnam

China managed to capture several Vietnamese towns near the Chinese Vietnamese border.

Devastated Vietnamese Town

After three weeks and six days, China withdrew, claiming victory. Vietnam claimed China was driven out and they too claimed victory.

February 18

Snow falls over the Sahara Desert.

April 4

Pakistan
President Bhutto hanged

This statement was read out to the condemned man in his cell.
"According to the March 18, 1978 order of the Lahore High Court, you, Mr Zulfikar Ali Bhutto, are to be hanged for the murder of Nawab Mohammad Ahmad Khan," read the order. "Your appeal in the Supreme Court was rejected on February 6, 1979, and the review petition was turned down on March 24, 1979. The president of Pakistan has decided not to interfere in this matter. So it has been decided to hang you."

Zulfikar Ali Bhutto

May 3

The 1979 United Kingdom general election was held to elect 635 members to the British House of Commons

The Conservative Party, led by Margaret Thatcher, ousted the incumbent Labour Government of James Callaghan with a parliamentary majority of 43 seats.

June 12

The Gossamer Albatross, with Bryan Allen as pilot, became the first human-powered aircraft to fly across the English Channel. The flight lasted 2 hours and 49 minutes and covered 36.2 kilometres between Folkestone, England, and Cap Gris Nez, France.

July 1

The metal-cased Walkman TPS-L2, the world's first low-cost personal stereo, went on sale in Japan. It was sold for around US$150.00. Sony predicted it would sell about 5,000 units a month, but it sold more than 30,000 in the first two months.

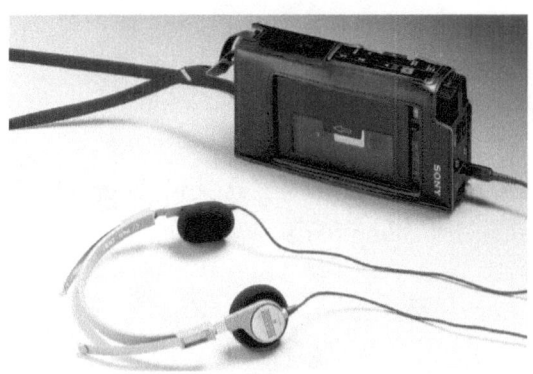

I attended a sales conference in Atlanta Georgia in January 1980. I then flew to London and Paris. On the return trip to Australia I met a lady in Business Class who was listening to her Walkman. I was amazed at the sound from such a small device.

I had a three-day stopover in Hong Kong. I purchased a Walkman, which changed the way I listened to music forever.

July 16

Hasan al-Bakr, President of Iraq resigns and hands over the keys to his deputy Saddam Hussein.

Happy Times

July 22

Ba'ath Party Purge

Saddam Hussein organised the arrest and later execution of nearly seventy members of his ruling party.

August 10

Michael Jackson released his breakthrough album *Off the Wall*. Seven million copies were sold in the U.S.A. alone. Over 20 million were sold worldwide.

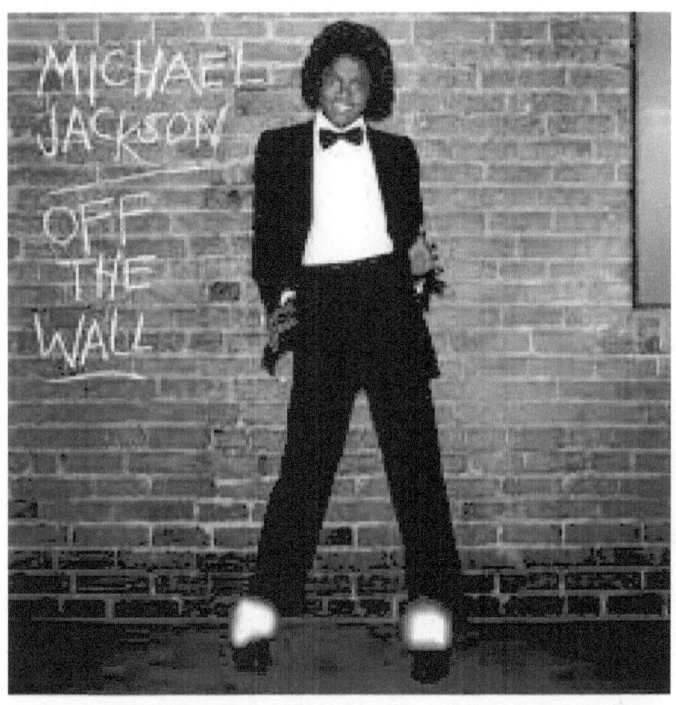

August 14

Fastnet Race

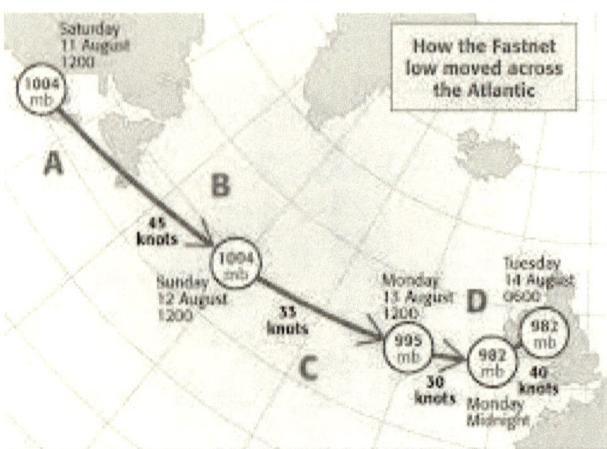

Fastnet is a famous ocean race that has been held by the Royal Ocean Racing Club every two years since 1925. It is a 605-mile course beginning in Cowes, rounding Fastnet Rock, and then sailing to Plymouth via the Isles of Scilly.

A severe storm on the third day of the race wreaked havoc on the 303-yacht fleet.

The storm claimed nineteen lives including four spectators.

Emergency Services, the Navy and many private vessels came to the fleet's aid. The Irish Navy were also involved in the rescue.

It became the largest peacetime rescue operation.

27 August

Lord Mountbatten's Assassination

Lord Mountbatten and Family Aboard *Shadow V*

Lord Mountbatten usually holidayed at his summer home, Classiebawn Castle, in Mullaghmore, a small seaside village in County Sligo, Ireland.

The village was only 12 miles from the border with Northern Ireland. In 1978, the IRA had allegedly attempted to shoot Mountbatten as he was aboard his boat, but choppy seas had prevented the sniper lining up his target accurately.

Despite security advice and warnings from the Irish police, on 27 August 1979, Mountbatten went lobster potting and tuna fishing in his 30-foot wooden boat, *Shadow V*, which had been moored in the harbour at Mullaghmore. IRA operative, Thomas McMahon, had slipped onto the unguarded boat that night and attached a radio-controlled bomb weighing 50 pounds. With Mountbatten aboard, just a few hundred yards from the shore, the bomb was detonated. The force of the blast destroyed the vessel; Mountbatten's legs were almost blown off. Local fishermen pulled Lord Mountbatten alive from the water; but he died from his injuries before arriving back at the shore. Also aboard the boat were his eldest daughter Patricia (Lady Brabourne), her husband John (Lord Brabourne), their twin sons Nicholas and Timothy, John's mother Doreen, Lady Brabourne, and Paul Maxwell, a young crew member from County Fermanagh. Nicholas aged 14, and Paul aged 15 were killed by the blast and the others were seriously injured. Lady Brabourne, aged 83 died from her injuries the following day.

The IRA issued a statement afterward, saying:

The IRA claim responsibility for the execution of Lord Louis Mountbatten. This operation is one of the discriminate ways we can bring to the attention of the English people the continuing occupation of our country. The death of Mountbatten and the tributes paid to him will be seen in sharp contrast to the apathy of the British government and the English people to the deaths of over three hundred British soldiers, and the deaths of Irish men, women and children at the hands of their forces.

Six weeks later, Sinn Féin vice-president Gerry Adams said of Mountbatten's death:

The IRA gave clear reasons for the execution. I think it is unfortunate that anyone has to be killed, but the furore created by Mountbatten's death showed up the hypocritical attitude of the media establishment. As a member of the House of Lords, Mountbatten was an emotional figure in both British and Irish politics. What the IRA did to him is what Mountbatten had been doing all his life to other people; and with his war record I don't think he could have objected to dying in what was clearly a war situation. He knew the danger involved in coming to this country. In my opinion, the IRA achieved its objective: people started paying attention to what was happening in Ireland.

September 16

The Great Escape

In the East German balloon escape in 1979, two families, with eight members in total, escaped the Eastern bloc country of East Germany by crossing the border to West Germany in a homemade hot air balloon. The escape happened at approximately 2:00 a.m. on 16 September 1979.

Peter Strelzyk was an East German Air Force mechanic who now worked as an electrician. Gunter Wetzel, who was a bricklayer by trade, worked with Peter in a plastics factory. They became very close friends.

The two men shared a common desire to escape the shackles of the communist regime in East Germany.

'Gunter, do you want to escape this place as much as I do?'

195

'Yes, more than anything I want my family to live in a free county.'

'Then let's start planning how we can escape. We must be very careful; the Stasi have spies everywhere.'

'Have you thought of how to get out, Peter?'

'One thought I had was we build a helicopter and fly out.'

'How did you come up with that idea?'

'I read an article in *Modern Mechanics*.'

'Okay, let's do some research.'

After two weeks of investigation it became obvious they would not be able to source a suitable reciprocating engine.

'Peter, I think we both agree a helicopter is out of the question.'

'Yes I agree, Gunther, but I have another idea which I believe is more practical.'

'What is it?'

'I watched a program on television last night on hot air balloons. I believe we could construct a balloon which would take all eight of us into West Germany.'

'Let's do our research and see if it's going to work.'

The pair began their research. The plan was to escape with their wives and total of four children (aged 2 to 15). They calculated the weight of the passengers and the craft itself to be around 750 kilograms. Subsequent calculations determined a balloon capable of lifting this weight would need to hold 2,000 cubic metres of air heated to 100 °C. The next calculation was the amount of material needed for the balloon, estimated at 800 square metres.

They travelled 50 kilometres from their hometown of Pob Neck top where they purchased 1-metre-wide rolls of cotton cloth totalling 850 metres in length at a department store after telling the astonished clerk that they needed the large quantity of material to use as tent lining for their camping club.

Wetzel spent two weeks sewing the cloth into a balloon-shaped bag, 15 metres wide by 20 metres long, on a 40-year-old manually operated sewing machine. Strelzyk spent the time building the gondola and burner assembly. The gondola was made from an iron frame, sheet metal floor, and clothesline run around the perimeter every 150 millimetres for the sides. The burner was made using two 11-kilogram bottles of liquid household gas, hoses, water pipe, a nozzle, and a piece of stove pipe.

April 1978

'I think we are ready to test the balloon, Gunther. Did you find a suitable site?'

'Yes I did, Peter; it's a forest near Ziegenruk.'

'A forest doesn't sound like a suitable site.'

'There is a large clearing; believe me it will be perfect.'

Ziegenruk is ten kilometres from the border.

They laid the balloon out on the grass and lit the burner. The balloon didn't inflate.

A few weeks later they found another site on a 25-metre cliff. They thought if they suspended the balloon vertically and lit the burner it would inflate. It didn't.

After a few more attempts they discovered the problem was the cotton material. It was too porous and leaked badly.

They decided on a synthetic taffeta as the material for balloon two.

So as not to arouse the attention of Stasi, they purchased the material in several stores up to 160 kilometres away.

Wetzel had acquired an electric sewing machine which made the task easier and much faster.

The two friends returned to the forest clearing where it took only five minutes to inflate the balloon. There was a problem, though. The burner was not producing enough heat to lift the balloon let alone the gondola with eight people.

'That's it. I've had enough, Peter. I'm going to look for another way to escape.'

'Don't give up now, Gunther—we're almost there.'

'We've almost been there for months; no, I'm out my friend.'

'I'll keep you posted on my progress.'

Strelzyk continued to experiment. In June 1979, he discovered that with the propane tank inverted, additional pressure caused the liquid propane to gasify which would create a bigger flame. He modified the gondola to mount the propane tanks upside down and returned to the test site where he found the new configuration produced a 12-metre-long flame. Strelzyk was ready to attempt an escape.

July 3
1 a.m.

The Strelzyk family lifted off from the forest clearing.

Everything was going to plan when they entered a large cloud. Atmospheric water vapour condensed on the balloon, which caused the balloon to descend.

They landed very close to the border and very close to a minefield. They managed to extricate themselves and sneak home.

Peter and Gunther conferred, and it was decided that Gunther and his family would rejoin the escape effort.

They also decided to double the size of the balloon to 4000 cubic metres and 25 metres in height.

They required 1,250 square metres of taffeta. Again, they purchased the material from a number of stores across the country.

They worked diligently for six weeks until at last they believed they had the transport that would deliver the two families across the border and a new life.

September 15

The balloon inflated in ten minutes, and they lifted off at 2 a.m. They did have some problems but nevertheless, they landed in Bavaria.

Both families enjoyed their newfound freedom in the west.

October 12

Cyclone Tip

Tip reached an intensity of 870 millibars; the lowest pressure recorded at sea level. It was the most powerful cyclone in history.

November 4

Iranian Hostage Crisis

Five hundred Iranian radical students invaded the American embassy in Tehran. Ninety hostages were taken. Fifty-three were U.S. diplomatic staff.

They were demanding the former Shah of Iran be returned to Iran to stand trial for crimes against the people. Their criminal actions were approved by the Ayatollah.

President Jimmie Carter lost the next election due to his failure to rescue the hostages although he tried.

Six American diplomats evaded capture and were rescued by a joint Canadian American team.

January 20, 1981

After negotiations Iran released the hostages minutes after President Ronald Regan was sworn in.

I was flying home from the U.K. when the captain announced that the plane taking the hostages home was about to pass us by. I was fortunate to be on the right side of the plane. The passengers erupted in applause. It was a very moving moment.

November 23

Dublin

Provisional IRA member Thomas McMahon was sentenced to life in prison for the assassination of Lord Mountbatten of Burma and three others.
He was released in 1990.

McMahon being taken away to prison

December 30

VisiCalc "visible calculator" is the first spreadsheet computer program for personal computers, originally released for Apple II by VisiCorp in 1979.... VisiCalc was considered to be Apple II's killer app. It sold over 700,000 copies in six years, and as many as 1 million copies over its history.

Dan Bricklin and Bob Frankston Co-Creators

EPILOGUE

Having written about the sixties and now the seventies I've realised every decade has its unique place in world history.

The 70s was a decade of change; particularly in an economic sense following the post war economic boom.

The social changes were also significant, including economic freedom for women. In 1979 Britain elected Margaret Thatcher as the first female Prime Minister

The oil crisis created an economic crisis around the world.

It was the author Tom Wolfe who coined the term "Me Decade" in his essay *The Me Decade and the Third Great Awakening*. It was published in New Yorker Magazine.

I hope this book will bring back memories, as I know the Fab 60s did for many readers.

Garry Willmott

THE END

First published 2022 by Crabtree Pty Ltd

Living in the Seventies is a work of fiction. Any resemblance to real persons, living or dead, is purely coincidental.

ISBN: 978-0-6451166-4-9 (p/b)
ISBN: 978-0-6451166-5-6 (ebook)

www.ingramcontent.com/pod-product-compliance
Lightning Source LLC
Chambersburg PA
CBHW030523020726
47494CB00004B/1213

* 9 7 8 0 6 4 5 1 1 6 6 4 9 *